Mom's PERFECT Boyfriend

"*Mom's Perfect Boyfriend* showcases author Crystal Hemmingway's genuine flair for originality and complete mastery of the romantic comedy genre." —*Midwest Book Review*

"*Mom's Perfect Boyfriend* is a modern must-read."
—*San Francisco Book Review*

"Sweet, funny, and totally original...I laughed out loud and flew through the pages!" —Kerry Winfrey, author of *Waiting for Tom Hanks*

"[A] charming romantic comedy...A refreshing escape with a futuristic twist." —*Foreword Reviews*

"Fans of Bridget Jones and Sophie Kinsella will love this fresh, original story...I couldn't put it down." —*Reader's Favorite*

"An incredibly fast and funny read." —*SheReads*

"A fun, bright and animated read." —*LoveReading*

"A cute and quirky story...Fast paced and funny."
—Danika Stone, Swoon Reads Winner and Author of *All the Feels*

"Delivers a powerful message couched in laughs...Hilarious."
—*Publishers Weekly*

"A funny, poignant debut." —*IndieReader*

Mom's PERFECT Boyfriend

Crystal Hemmingway

GALBADIA PRESS

Mom's Perfect Boyfriend by Crystal Hemmingway

First edition.

This is a work of fiction. Names, characters, places, and incidents either are the product of the author's imagination or are used fictitiously. Any resemblance to actual persons, living or dead, events, or locales is entirely coincidental.

All brand names and product names mentioned in this book are trademarks, registered trademarks, and trade names of their respective holders. Mention of a company name does not constitute endorsement. The author is not associated with any product or vendor mentioned in this book.

PUBLISHER'S CATALOGING-IN-PUBLICATION DATA
Names: Hemmingway, Crystal, author.
Title: Mom's perfect boyfriend / Crystal Hemmingway.
Series: Smart Companions.
Description: Austin, TX: Galbadia Press, 2019.
Identifiers: ISBN 978-1-950458-00-4 (Hardcover) | 978-1-950458-01-1 (pbk.) | 978-1-950458-02-8 (ebook)
Subjects: LCSH Mothers and daughters--Fiction. | Family--Fiction. | Robots--Fiction. | Love stories. | Epistolary fiction. | Romance fiction. | BISAC FICTION / Romance / Romantic Comedy
Classification: LCC PS3608.E4775 M66 2019| DDC 813.6--dc23

www.galbadiapress.com

MOM'S PERFECT BOYFRIEND

AUTHOR'S NOTE

This story is true. I assembled it from my text messages, emails, and journal entries. I know it's hard to believe. I don't know if I'll ever be able to explain some of the things I experienced.

Names have been changed to protect the innocent (and because I don't want to get sued). "Boople" is a very real global tech company with a fleet of lawyers. Please don't sue me, Boople lawyers.

To offer a broader perspective, I have included excerpts from my mom's diary. Technically, I never got her permission to publish it – or even read it. Actually, it'd be better off if she never found out about this book.

In conclusion: true story, please don't sue me, please don't tell my mom.

-C.H.

BOOPLE CHAT, THURS JUN 29, 7:32 PM

Crystal:	soooo excited for hawaii!!!
Crystal:	think you'll be home soon?
David:	they just found another critical bug on my level
David:	it's going to be a late night
Crystal:	aw i'm sorry
Crystal:	i can help you pack
David:	thanks i'd appreciate it
David:	i really need this vacation
Crystal:	we'll make it our best yet ;)

TEXT MESSAGES, JUNE 29

Mom:	Hey, Sweetie. Do you have a minute to chat?
Crystal:	Sure, I can talk while I pack. Can I call you in 10 min?
Mom:	That would be great.

BOOPLE CHAT, FRI JUNE 30, 1:15 AM

Crystal:	hey
Lisa:	hi
Lisa:	aren't you leaving for hawaii in like 4 hours?
Crystal:	i just got off a three hour phone call with mom
Crystal:	she kind of invited herself on our trip
Lisa:	again?
Crystal:	i tried to tell her no but she wouldn't listen

Lisa:	she's not your responsibility
Lisa:	you can't be her best friend forever
Crystal:	i know but it's too late now ☹
Crystal:	she already bought the ticket
Lisa:	well then good luck
Lisa:	you're going to need it

EMAIL, JUNE 30

From: Maui Turtle Tours <amanda@mauiturtletours.com>
To: Crystal Hemmingway <crystalkitty_01@booplemail.com>
Subject: Re: Trip for Three

Aloha Crystal!

I have cancelled and rebooked your trip as you requested. I have attached an invoice with the updated balance. Please review the information below and feel free to call or email with any questions.

Hope you have a wonderful time here in Maui!

Mahalo,
Amanda S.

Cancelled*:
- 1 x Beachside Couples' Massage
- 1 x Beginner Surfing Lesson (Private), 2 adults
- 1 x Zipline Tour, 2 adults

- 2 x Maui Burlesque Cabaret Show tickets
- 1 x Candlelit Yacht Dinner for two

Booked:

- 1 x Snorkeling Adventure Tour, 3 adults
- 1 x Dolphin Cruise (lunch included), 3 adults
- 1 x Maui Pineapple Ranch entry tickets, 3 adults
- 3 x Deluxe Fire Dancing Luau tickets (1 vegetarian, 2 omnivore)

All cancellations and rebookings may be subject to a fee, up to 50% of the cost of the tour, if requested by the guest less than 24 hours before the date of service. Cancellations and rebookings due to weather and other unforeseen circumstances will be made free of charge.

TEXT MESSAGES, JULY 6

Crystal:	hey are you coming?
Crystal:	we set sail in 2 min
David:	i'm going to sit this one out
Crystal:	everything ok?
David:	yeah i just need some time alone

BOOPLE CHAT, SAT JULY 8 10:32 AM

Crystal:	can i call you?
Lisa:	give me 15 min?
Crystal:	k

Lisa:	you alright?
Crystal:	david wants a break
Crystal:	like from our relationship
Lisa:	calling now

TEXT MESSAGES, JULY 8

Mom:	Happy Saturday!
Crystal:	Thanks Mom, you too. ☺
Mom:	Any plans this weekend?
Crystal:	Unpack and do laundry. :P
Mom:	Same here! And a walk with Ingrid tomorrow.
Crystal:	Sounds good. ☺
Mom:	Missing the Hawaii weather already.
Crystal:	Yep it was nice
Mom:	It was so kind of you and David to include me. It was a wonderful trip, and I'm so glad I finally got a chance to see Maui. Thank you so much! <3 I'm so proud of you and excited to hear more about your novel. Love you so much!
Crystal:	Thanks, I enjoyed it, too. Won't be much to show on the novel for awhile. Love you too. <3
Mom:	Bye! Say hi to David for me!
Crystal:	Thanks, I will, bye. ☺

MARGOT'S JOURNAL, SUNDAY JULY 9

I had a great weekend. I flew back from Hawaii on Friday night, so I slept in on Saturday. We had a great time in Hawaii, and I think Crystal and David enjoyed it, too. There was a mix-up at the hotel, so they upgraded us to the honeymoon suite! It was so nice that we could all stay in the same room. I've never stayed anywhere that fancy, not even when I went to that dentists' conference with my ex-husband. This place was much better, and right on the beach. The view was to die for.

We packed a lot in on the trip, but I wouldn't have minded a few more days. We still managed to squeeze in snorkeling, a dolphin cruise, plenty of shopping, a luau, some hikes, a surf competition (as spectators), horseback riding, a few movies, some ice cream, and a lot of great meals. Crystal is still doing the vegetarian thing, so we looked for places with options for her. David was a bit down this trip, and it looked like he'd put on a bit of weight, too. It sounded like his last video game project was very stressful, but he just finished it. I hope they treat him better on the next one.

It was hard to come home to overcast weather after all that Hawaiian sun, but it was nice to be back in my own place and eating my own food. I got the house cleaned up a bit, and ran a bunch of errands. I had a nice walk with Ingrid, although she's a bit depressed right now. Her husband is dealing with a lot of health problems, and she doesn't have a lot of people to talk to. I'm trying to be supportive, but I hope she can find a way to be more positive soon.

After the walk, I did some grocery shopping at the farmers' market and two different grocery stores. Then I cooked everything up for the week, so my meals are all ready to go. It's going to be another busy week, and I always feel better when I eat my own food. My pants are also a little tight after the trip (must've been all the ice cream! Hehe!), so I'll have to cut back a little there.

Tonight, I went online to post some photos from the trip. I didn't mean to, but I saw a post from James, and then I looked at his profile. It looks like he bought a new car – a red corvette with black interior. Why didn't he get that earlier? I had to ride in his beat-up old Corolla. I know I shouldn't have even looked, but it's still hard to see pictures of him with that skinny new girlfriend, both happy and smiling. I thought James and I really had a connection, but now it's like I was never even there. I'll have to work on releasing those feelings, because the yoga and meditation don't seem to have cleared them yet. Maybe another month will be enough.

Then I saw a picture of Lisa and Bryan and his parents at brunch. Lisa never goes to brunch with me. I know we're not in the same town, but we could be. I guess I don't understand why they live near his parents and not me, and why we can't be the kind of family that brunches.

I also got an invite to the Helping Hands Housewife Association (HHHA) holiday fundraiser. Mother is in charge again, and it would probably be good for me to go. I'll have to check with the girls on their holiday plans, because the fundraiser is on Christmas eve this year.

It's going to be a good week. I'm going to focus on being compassionate toward my patients, especially those with halitosis and gingivitis.

Gratitudes:
1. I am grateful for the unexpected Hawaiian vacation.
2. I am grateful for Crystal and Lisa.
3. I am grateful for my job, which deepens my appreciation of vacations.

BOOPLE CHAT, MONDAY, JULY 10 2:13 PM

Crystal:	yo
Crystal:	has mom been texting you like every five minutes?
Crystal:	like photos of her coworkers and her food and stuff?
Lisa:	YES
Lisa:	i stopped responding an hour ago and it's still going
Crystal:	i think it's withdrawal from the trip
Lisa:	probably
Crystal:	did she ask you about christmas?
Lisa:	yeah
Crystal:	i know she wants to get her tickets early but still
Crystal:	it's half a year away
Lisa:	yeah

Lisa:	we're doing the usual Fontana christmas
Crystal:	at bryan's parents' place?
Lisa:	yup
Lisa:	i told mom we haven't made plans yet
Crystal:	so she'll be on her own then?
Lisa:	we could invite her, but she didn't seem to have very much fun last year
Crystal:	yeah better not to
Crystal:	well at least we've got some time to think about it
Crystal:	i can't deal with december right now
Crystal:	it's hard enough just getting through the week
Crystal:	since my future is still a giant question mark
Lisa:	you mean david?
Crystal:	yeah
Lisa:	have you talked to him yet?
Crystal:	no
Crystal:	i thought about emailing him, but i don't even know what to say
Lisa:	do you still love him?
Crystal:	of course
Lisa:	do you want to get back together?
Crystal:	i think so...but it's not like i can just disown mom, either
Crystal:	i don't think "i'm sorry" is going to be enough
Crystal:	our relationship won't work the way things are currently
Lisa:	well all relationships require compromise
Lisa:	but it doesn't all have to be on you, either

Crystal:	thanks
Crystal:	i do think there are some things i want to change though
Crystal:	i can't be mom's companion for the rest of my adult life
Crystal:	what she really needs is a boyfriend or husband, someone to be with her 24/7
Lisa:	yeah
Lisa:	is she still online dating?
Crystal:	no she quit
Crystal:	she told me on the trip that she wants to "leave it up to fate"
Lisa:	again?
Crystal:	it might work
Lisa:	it hasn't for a decade
Lisa:	seriously...she needs to find someone before she drives us both insane
Crystal:	i know
Lisa:	bryan and i have had talks about this
Crystal:	really?
Lisa:	yeah
Lisa:	it's why i fly in twice a year, for two days at a time
Lisa:	it's exhausting but i think we both enjoy it more that way
Crystal:	but mom is only two hours away from me by car
Lisa:	true but you still have choices
Crystal:	so what do you recommend?
Lisa:	start setting boundaries

Crystal:	like limiting phone calls to two hours or less?
Lisa:	plan them up against other commitments, even if they're imaginary
Lisa:	and you don't have to respond to her texts right away, either
Crystal:	but if i don't then i keep thinking about it and it stresses me out
Lisa:	don't even look at your phone
Crystal:	what if it's an emergency?
Lisa:	she'd find a way
Lisa:	she could email you, make an actual call...there are plenty of ways
Crystal:	oh right
Crystal:	yeah, i think i'll feel better once i have a plan
Crystal:	i just wish mom didn't have such ridiculously high standards
Lisa:	yeah
Lisa:	i don't think anyone can meet ALL her expectations
Crystal:	i wish we could just buy her a made-to-order boyfriend or something
Lisa:	if only

TECHBEAT ARTICLE, JULY 11

Would You Shag a Robot?

Ever wish you had a robot to do your dishes? Drive you to work? Keep you warm at night? That future may be closer than you think.

Boople has announced an experimental program of robotic "Smart Companions," which the company claims are "designed for domestic use." As the program is still in the research stage, Boople reps are closed to questions, but a source close to the company says there is "a strong possibility" that they will resemble humans, and emulate human behaviors.

The Smart Companion team is led by Dr. Paul Devereux, the leading AI psychologist who recently published *Robots Have Feelings Too: Essays on Technology, Psychology, and Love*. Boople clearly wants us to invite these Smart Companions not just into our homes, but also our hearts. Good luck with that, Dr. Devereux.

EMAILS, JULY 11

From: Crystal Hemmingway <crystalkitty_01@booplemail.com>
To: Margot Hemmingway <margot.hemmingway@boople-mail.com>
Subject: Heads Down at Work

Dear Mom,

We're prepping the holiday catalogs at work, so I'm going to be working some long hours.

Unfortunately, this means that I'll have to limit our phone calls to once a week, two hours or less. Sorry, I know it's a big shift for us. ☹

I had a great time in Hawaii and love you very much.

Thanks for understanding.

Love,
Crystal

EMAIL, JULY 11

From: Crystal Hemmingway <crystalkitty_01@booplemail.com>
To: David Richards <darth_david@booplemail.com>
Subject: Hey

Hey David,

Hope you are doing well. I'm really sorry again about Hawaii, and how stressful it was. After all your hard work on *MOB2*, I know you deserved a week to just chill.

I've been thinking a lot about what you said, and how I act around Mom. I want you to know that I want to change – not just for you, but for me as well. It's going to be a process, and I can't promise it'll be different in a day, or even a month. But I've got a plan, and I've already started the first step. I emailed

Mom this morning and told her that I'm limiting our phone calls to once a week.

Also, I have some mail for you. I don't know if you want me to forward it somewhere, or keep it here for now. I could also hide it in the yard somewhere, if you prefer to pick it up when I'm not around.

Talk to you later,
Crystal

P.S. Do you know how long you'll be in Hawaii?

MARGOT'S JOURNAL, TUESDAY JULY 11

Today was a little challenging. I left the office early to volunteer at a career fair at Cypress High School (Grace Sommer's daughter, Alice, goes there). They didn't have any representation in dental care, so I thought I'd help Grace out (she's the PTA committee chair).

They were supposed to have a neurosurgeon at the fair as well, but he got called away to an emergency, so I was the only one from any healthcare-related field. Dozens of students wanted to know how to get in to medical school, but no one wanted to know what it was like to be a dental hygienist.

I don't suppose I can expect them to be interested. Teenagers are under a lot of pressure, and at that age they tend to be very self-centered. Of course I'd already decided on my career choice by 14, but kids these days seem to be a lot more indecisive. It's probably the internet, with sites like YouTube giving them ideas about being professional video game players. David said there's a special name for them. Something party-related, like "banners" or "streamers." Apparently these kids just sit at home all day, and people pay them for some reason. If this keeps up, who's going to be around to clean teeth?

Of course, Grace brought Alice over to say "hello." Alice is a junior now. Grace told me all about how Alice is the top of her class. Lisa and Crystal were both valedictorians, but of course I was too polite to say that. Grace's daughter has had a rough year, because she's highly sensitive and has several food allergies, including eggs, peanuts, soy, corn, and gluten. I told them about some allergy-free chocolate chips I'd found at Whole Foods, but of course she already knew about them, and her private chef uses them all the time. Grace likes to say that she had to hire the chef (and the house cleaners and the grocery shoppers and the lawn care and the dog walker) because she's simply too busy, but she doesn't work for a living. She's divorced like me, but Alice's father is an incredibly wealthy plastic surgeon. It seems he pays Grace quite a generous alimony, because she still has the lifestyle of a rich housewife.

Of course, Grace doesn't see it that way. She's always stressed and overwhelmed, because she's president of the Greater San Diego HHHA, the PTA chair, Alice's driver, a part-time yoga teacher, a wellness coach... the list goes on. She has a soap-making business, too. She's at the farmers' market every weekend, selling her beautiful handmade goats' milk soaps from goats in an underprivileged country. It's Grace's way of "giving back."

Not that I'm jealous. At least, not about the money. It would be nice, but I do well enough. It was easier when the girls' father was around, but I put them both through college, and they didn't want for much. And now I get to live in San Diego, and this is not a cheap city.

Then Grace has to go and tell me how close she and Alice are. And how they are just the best of friends, and even when Alice is at school, they still text throughout the day. As she was saying this, Alice gives her a huge hug, to rub it all in.

I don't understand why Lisa and Crystal aren't like that. I thought we were close, but once they left for college, it was "Adios, Mom." Both of them went out of state, when it would've been much cheaper and easier to go to a state university. But I wanted the best for them, and so I let them go. I thought that if I gave them space, they'd recognize the sacrifices I made for them someday, and they'd come back to me.

Instead, I get 48-hour visits from Lisa, and now this email from Crystal, telling me that she's limiting my contact with her to a two-hour phone call, once a week.

When I read it, it was like a knife through my heart. After we had such a great time in Hawaii, too. I understand that she's busy with work, but I'm busy, too. So now I have to contact her on her terms, when it's convenient for her.

Can I even text her anymore? I don't know.

Surely, email is safe. Or will I have to ask her permission, too?

I'd expect this kind of treatment if I'd wronged her, but I've given her nothing but love and support.

Maybe she's going through something right now. Problems at work, maybe? She didn't seem to want to talk about work much on the trip. And she looked like she'd gained a little weight since last year, too.

I want to be compassionate and give her space, but this really hurts. I always made sure she and Lisa had everything they needed. All the summer day camps, lessons, school events. I didn't miss a single one.

And now I get two hours a week?

Am I going to have to start making lists of things to tell her? What if I forget something important? Would she even want me to text her if something bad happened to her grandmother?

I should probably do some yoga, and some deep breathing. I have to bake four dozen cookies tonight. Our office building is having a bake sale on Saturday to raise money for victims of the hurricane on the East Coast. No one from our office volunteered, so I said I'd bring some cookies. I thought it'd be a couple dozen, but they wanted 12 dozen (144), which is why I have to start tonight. I thought I'd bake them tonight and tomorrow, and then frost them Friday night. I have yoga on Thursday, so that only leaves me with three days.

I'm going to think positive thoughts for Crystal. She must really be hurting right now to send an email like that, so I can only hope that she'll be more communicative when she gets through this. I just wish she'd lean on me so we could work through it together.

Gratitudes:
1. I am grateful for my daughters, and for the opportunities they give me to grow.
2. I am grateful to Grace for inviting me to the career fair, for the opportunity to influence young minds.
3. I am grateful for yogic breathing, so I could remain calm in challenging situations like I faced today.

EMAIL, JULY 12

From: Grateful Goats Soaps <grace@gratefulgoatssoaps.com>
To: Margot Hemmingway <margot.hemmingway@boople-mail.com>
Subject: A Gift for You

Hello Gorgeous,

Just in time for summer, we are now offering our most delicious scent yet: Kona Coconut. Straight from the shores of Hawaii, our fair trade Kona Coffee beans are ground by hand and mixed with organic coconut oils. Kona Coconut will carry you off to the white beaches of Hawaii, and turn your daily bath or shower into a spa paradise.

In need of a little detox? Try our new exfoliating soap, made from organic, gluten-free oats and rice bran. We set out to make an effective exfoliating soap free from harmful plastic microbeads, which wreak havoc on our lakes, rivers, oceans. Our organic rice bran is just as effective, and safe for both you and the earth.

We're confident you'll love these soaps, which is why we're offering you a free trial bar of each. Just bring the attached coupon to our booth at the farmers' market to claim your free gift.

Love and Light,
Grace <3

Grateful Goats Soaps. Clean body, clear conscience. Proceeds benefit Himalayan Sherpas.

BOOPLE CHAT, WEDS JULY 12, 5:22 PM

Lisa:	how's it going?
Crystal:	alright
Crystal:	glad i have work right now to distract me from the whole david thing
Lisa:	still no response to your email?
Crystal:	nope
Crystal:	i thought he'd be home by now
Crystal:	or at least have internet access
Lisa:	aw

Crystal:	i'm trying to give him space
Crystal:	but i just wish he would've given me some answers, you know?
Crystal:	like what does he mean by "break"? and when is he coming home?
Lisa:	yeah
Crystal:	i moved some of his stuff into the closet, so i don't have to look at it
Crystal:	every time i think about my future with him, my stomach feels all wobbly
Lisa:	aw ☹
Crystal:	i think i'd go crazy without work
Crystal:	i've been distracting myself with tv in the evenings
Crystal:	but after a week of this i'm starting to feel like a slacker
Lisa:	well you've been through a lot
Crystal:	yeah thanks
Lisa:	it sucks that he didn't explain the break thing
Crystal:	yeah
Crystal:	i mean it's nice that there's hope
Crystal:	but it's the silence that kills me
Lisa:	☹

CRYSTAL'S JOURNAL, JULY 15

I haven't had a single text message from Mom in three days. It's been pretty strange, to be honest. I kept checking my phone, expecting something to be there, but there was nothing. I even went on Facebook yesterday to see if she posted anything (she had), which was a relief because then I knew nothing bad had happened to her.

The good news is that I've been amazingly productive these last few days. As part of my new Life Improvement Plan (LIP for short), I decided to stop slacking at work. No more endless checking of the email (personal and work). No more social media, and no more loitering in Boople Chat. I used to just keep Boople Chat open all day, and I'd tell David all the silly things, like when I got free cookies or what color socks my friend Jen was wearing (she has a quite a collection). I realized that I was starting to do that to Lisa instead (post-David), and I decided it was time to stop. It was majorly distracting, and sometimes I wouldn't even start on my work in earnest until after lunch.

But no more!

I think I've gotten more done in the past three days than I did all last week. I'm a little worried that my boss will notice and expect me to keep up this pace, but maybe that would be a good thing. Put some pressure on me to avoid those distractions.

Too bad they don't pay based on my output. But maybe they'll notice and give me a raise... but reviews won't come around again until next summer, so it's probably wishful thinking.

Ah, well. This isn't about the money, anyway. It's about owning the day, and making my dreams come true.

Speaking of which!

I actually dusted off the novel again. I read it over earlier this week, and it's pretty bad. As in, probably not worth salvaging. The concept was a Rapunzel retelling, but a lot of it just wasn't working. It was really stiff and didn't make a lot of sense. But I had a stroke of inspiration the other day, and I think I have a better idea for how to rewrite it. I'm only 4300 words in at the moment, but it seems to be working a lot better. If I can just keep up this pace, I'll be on track to finish in a few months. Then I could finally say that I finished something, which would be great.

I've also been thinking more about what David said, especially about how I change my appearance around Mom. I think I knew on some level that I was doing it, but I didn't realize just how much until I compared the Hawaii vacation photos to my usual photos with David. In Hawaii, I was dressing like I did in high school. I let my hair air dry, and mostly wore a baggy windbreaker and convertible nylon pants. Some of that is the climate, but still. If it was just me and David, I probably would've worn some cuter clothes, and I definitely wouldn't have felt the need to wear a rash guard at the beach.

I wasn't exactly on a bikini diet and workout plan, but I did buy a new two-piece for the trip. But then I found out that Mom was going to come, and I realized that I'm a few pounds heavier than last time she saw me. I think it's only five pounds or so, but when I gained the Freshman 15, she told me, "I'll love you no matter what size you are." I weighed 130 pounds! It wasn't like I'd ballooned to the size of a whale. And since I'm around 135 now, I *definitely* didn't want a repeat of that incident. So my bikini never saw the light of day, and I never got to show it off to David.

I'm still not sure where David and I will stand, but I've decided that it's time to acknowledge who I am, and how I want to dress. So I wore my only pair of heels to work the other day, just for fun. But on the way in, the heel got stuck in a grate, and snapped right off. I had my backup flats on before I even sat at my desk, but it felt like a sign. I've had those heels since my high school band concerts, and now seemed like a good time for an upgrade.

So on the way home from work yesterday, I took a detour to Saks.

Not the outlet – actual Saks. And I tried on some legit heels. Like Manolos and Louboutins (I still don't know how you even pronounce it). I walked in there with my pre-loved Gucci purse and tried to hold my head up high. The shoe salesman was really nice, and even offered some suggestions when I (reluctantly) admitted that the Manolos and Louboutins were uncomfortable. He brought out this pair of heeled Prada sandals, and oh my god they were the most beautiful shoes I'd even seen. I was sure they'd be horrendously uncomfortable, but they weren't at all. In fact, they were more comfortable than my trusty high school Rockports, even though the heels were over an inch taller.

The only problem? The price. They're almost $600, and will probably never go on sale. So I put them on hold, and then came home and turned the internet upside down looking for a discount.

But guess what?

Designer shoes aren't just expensive, they're also rare. I couldn't find a single site that had the same style, color, and size in stock. So even if I could use a promo code, it probably won't be for the right pair.

Which leaves me with a dilemma.

Do I buy these perfect, amazing shoes and get one step closer to becoming the sophisticated lady I've always wanted to be?

Or do I take the sensible route, and go back to Macy's and consignment shops like usual? Well, I know which one Mom would pick. But that doesn't mean I should drop hundreds on a single pair of shoes, either.

What if a friend's dog chewed them up? Or what if they fell in a manhole? $600, down the drain.

But on the other hand, I just spent over $1500 on a trip to Hawaii (and that was just my half). The ticket alone was almost the entire cost of the shoes. And what did I get?

Dumped and miserable, that's what.

I could've bought almost three pairs of Prada sandals for that, and they probably would've made me *much* happier.

I can see why they call it "retail therapy." I'm going to sleep on this, because that's the smart thing to do. Even if they do offer free returns.

The prince pulled Rapunzel into the empty dining room, and shut the door carefully behind him. Rapunzel's heart was beating fast, and her stomach clenched in anticipation. Why wouldn't he meet her gaze? Had something gone terribly wrong?

Finally, he spoke.

"I can't do this," he said.

"That's fine," Rapunzel said. "I'll make the necessary apologies to the duchess. We can say you've taken ill."

He didn't reply. Slowly, he pulled his gaze back to hers. His expression was desperate, the pitiable look of a caged animal.

"It's not about the dinner," she said, as the pieces finally fell into place.

It was about the engagement, just as she feared. Rapunzel's mind raced. She'd risked everything to come here, and he wanted break off the engagement *now*? He was the one who came to her tower in the first place, and convinced her to leave. And now that she had barely started living, was it all going to just...end?

"It's over, then?" Rapunzel forced herself to choke out the words. She had to be sure.

"I'm sorry," he said. "I never meant..."

Rapunzel nodded slowly. She placed a hand on a nearby chair to steady herself. It felt as if the floor could open up and swallow her whole, but she forced herself to stand upright, trying to take the news with the grace of a princess.

Of course, there was probably no point now. The prince was rejecting her. So she was, and always would be, a commoner.

"I'll be out of the palace by first light," she said. "Unless you wish me to leave immediately?"

The prince studied her face, as if the thought of her leaving the palace only just occurred to him.

"First light, then," she said.

"I take my leave, your highness," she added. The formal address felt odd even as she spoke it, because to her, he was merely "William." Even when she found out his true identity, he insisted that she never use his formal titles.

That was all going to change now. He was her sovereign prince, and nothing more.

Rapunzel strode toward the door and left, forcing herself not to glance back. She wove through the hallways, holding her head high. Servants curtsied to her, and she nodded in acknowledgement.

By tomorrow they'll barely spare me a glance, she thought.

When she finally reached her room, she went to her writing desk. It took her sixteen attempts, but finally she managed to write a passable letter to her mother, Dame Gothel. How angry she must've been, to discover how Rapunzel had fled the tower. She hadn't heard a word from Rapunzel, and the guilt of her escape pressed on Rapunzel each day.

She had imagined, from time to time, writing a special letter to accompany her wedding invitation. Rapunzel thought that her mother might forgive her, if she knew her daughter had a promising future ahead. Rapunzel never thought she'd have to swallow her pride now, and beg for Dame Gothel's forgiveness.

Rapunzel sealed the letter with wax, and gave it to a servant. With luck, her mother would arrive before first light.

If she forgave her.

Rapunzel didn't even want to think about the alternative. She wanted nothing more than to disappear, not spend a life begging for scraps in the capital's grimy streets – or worse. No one would want to touch the woman discarded by the prince – the would-be princess who presumed far beyond her station.

Later that night, as Rapunzel lay awake in the extravagant palace bed, she wondered why the tears didn't come. She was covered in layer upon layer of sumptuous quilts, and yet she felt numb with cold.

I never belonged here, she thought. It was all a terrible, beautiful dream.

EMAIL, JULY 15

From: Peggy Hemmingway <phemmingway@hhha.org>

To: Margot Hemmingway <margot.hemmingway@boople-mail.com>
Subject: Hi from Northfield

Dear Margot,

How is life in sunny California? Hot and humid here in Northfield...high 80s...lots of mosquitoes.

Set the date for the HHHA Holiday Fundraiser...hall was booked out so we're on the 24th...later than usual. Would love if you could make it.

Heard your old friend Eric Robertson and his wife have separated...might be a divorce before Christmas.

How are your girls? Has Crystal set a date yet? Looking forward to the wedding.

Love you much.
Mother

P.S. Would like to be friends with a gal on Facebook. She has verbally agreed but now need to locate her on the website.

EMAIL, JULY 15

From: Margot Hemmingway <margot.hemmingway@boople-mail.com>
To: Peggy Hemmingway <phemmingway@hhha.org>

Subject: Re: Hi from Northfield

Dear Mother,

Sorry about the humid weather. Hope you get some cool breezes soon.

San Diego is a little hotter than usual this year, high 90's this week. Next week it might get as high as 100, which is rare for us.

I will check with the girls and see what the holiday plans are like this year. The HHHA fundraisers are always a treat so I would hate to miss it.

As far as I know, Crystal hasn't set a date yet. Both she and Lisa are working long hours right now, so we don't get to talk as often as we'd like. Hopefully work will slow down for them again soon, so Crystal can start preparations. I'd very much like to help, but she also mentioned hiring a planner, so she might go that route.

Hope the fundraiser planning goes well.

Love,
Margot

P.S. To find your friend on Facebook, type her name in the search box on your Facebook home page. If you have any difficulties, call me and I'd be happy to walk you through it.

EMAIL, JULY 17

From: Crystal Hemmingway <chemmingway@princessesinc.com>
To: Jennifer Smith <jennifers@princessesinc.com>
Subject: Re: Desert Palace Playset (Item #A4405938)

Hi Jen,

Thanks for your feedback. I removed the term "your princess" to avoid a potential gender bias, and added in the imagination reference as well.

Here's the updated version:

"Tucked away in the heart of a magical desert, this palace is an oasis fit for a princess. Join Talia, the Arabian Princess, and her friends in this three-tiered castle filled with lights, sounds, and imagination. Includes six figurines, furniture, and accessories for hours of fun."

Let me know what you think.

Thanks,
Crystal

EMAIL, JULY 17

From: David Richards <darth_david@booplemail.com>
To: Crystal Hemmingway <crystalkitty_01@booplemail.com>
Subject: Re: Hey

Hey Crystal,

Sorry about the way we left things in Hawaii. I didn't want you to have to fly home alone, but I needed some time on my own to process everything, and I wanted to be surrounded by nature.

It's good to hear that you're setting some limits with your mother, and that you're doing it for you. It was hard to see you getting so stressed out after her phone calls, when you already have a stressful job and so much else going on. I know that you care about her, and that's part of what I like about you, but it's important to take care of yourself, too.

I got an email from Mike the other day. He's going to take a leave of absence from NASA and finally hike the Pacific Crest Trail (PCT). He's been preparing for the last few months, and is heading out in the next week. It was something we'd always talked about doing together, but we never could find the right time.

Then I emailed work to request an extra week off. Turns out I finally earned my sabbatical, but the benefit is being discontinued at the end of the year. So if I don't take the time this year, I lose it.

Mike and I got to talking, and he invited me to do the PCT with him. He talks about it like it's going to be some epic Tolkienesque adventure, trekking through forests, climbing snow-capped mountains, and sleeping under the stars. I know it seems crazy, because I'm not really the outdoorsy type, but that's why I think this is exactly what I need. *MOB2* was a train wreck, and I can't imagine spending the rest of my working career on the verge of burnout. A few months in nature might help me find some answers. Or at least help me get in shape again.

It's probably going to take us five months, and I'm nowhere near fit enough. From everything Mike told me, this may be the hardest thing we've ever done, but that's why I think I need to do it. If all goes well, we'll both be better people at the other end of the trail. But I don't want to ask you to wait for me, because I probably won't be the same person when I return.

In the meantime, I'll be going off the grid for awhile, so I'm sending the apartment office a check. I'm covering my rent for the next half of the year, so you won't have to move. I'll think about the best way to handle my stuff, but in the meantime, feel free to rearrange things how you like. And if there's an emergency, my parents will know how to reach me.

I'm sorry that you got caught up in the middle of all this. I just need some time on my own to figure things out.

-David

P.S. As for the mail, if you could forward anything time-sensitive to my parents, I'd appreciate it. I'll update my addresses to their place so you shouldn't have to deal with it for long.

BOOPLE CHAT, TUES JULY 18, 9:45 AM

Crystal: i bought the shoes
Lisa: waaaagh! send me a picture
Crystal: ok just emailed it
Lisa: who emails photos? just paste it here you dork
Crystal: too late
Lisa: OMG those are stunning
Crystal: they'd better be...i spent way too much on them
Lisa: how much?
Crystal: ugggggghhh...you really don't want to know
Lisa: isn't saks the best?
Crystal: YES
Crystal: i could get used to being called "miss" and being offered fiji water
Lisa: LOL
Crystal: this is awful
Crystal: i'll never be able to shop at old navy again
Lisa: welcome to the dark side ;)
Crystal: this is all your fault
Lisa: i've never spent more than $300 on a pair of shoes
Crystal: that's ten times what a pair of shoes should cost
Lisa: says the girl wearing $600 heels

Crystal: hey how did you know that?

Lisa: oh was i right? nice

Crystal: not cool

Lisa: stop feeling guilty and own it

Lisa: not like you can return them now

Crystal: don't remind me

Crystal: gotta run, meeting

Lisa: kk

BOOPLE CHAT, TUES JULY 18, 12:05 PM

Crystal: hey

Lisa: must've been some meeting

Crystal: um yeah...they're shutting down our office

Lisa: WHAT?

Crystal: yeah, i'm out of a job

Lisa: oh my god, i'm so sorry

Crystal: yeah it sucks

Crystal: we had record sales this year, too, but they decided to outsource all our jobs

Lisa: that doesn't make any sense

Lisa: there's no way some random outsourcer can write product descriptions as well as you

Crystal: tell that to the CEO

Lisa: ☹

Crystal: sorry i don't mean to take it out on you

Lisa: it's fine

Crystal: can i call you?

Lisa:	i've got a meeting for the next hour, but right afterwards?
Crystal:	ok, thanks
Lisa:	we can still chat here if you want...it's just a conference call
Crystal:	thanks, that'd be nice
Lisa:	of course
Lisa:	wish i could give you a hug
Crystal:	yeah where's david when i need him
Lisa:	☹
Crystal:	he's in canada now btw
Lisa:	?
Crystal:	he's going to hike the PCT
Lisa:	doesn't that take months?
Crystal:	yep
Crystal:	he's on a journey of self-discovery
Lisa:	aw man
Crystal:	yeah it's not ideal
Crystal:	but at least he's sending along his half of the rent
Crystal:	so i won't be homeless on his account
Lisa:	that's good at least
Crystal:	but now i'm starting to regret these shoes
Lisa:	aw
Crystal:	$600 is like a months' rent
Crystal:	maybe i should consign them
Lisa:	it's not worth it
Lisa:	you love those shoes
Lisa:	and consignment will give you peanuts

Crystal:	TRUE
Crystal:	yeah i guess i'm stuck with them for now ;)
Lisa:	☺
Lisa:	i can get you a reference at boople if you're interested
Lisa:	we've got some technical writing jobs open
Crystal:	thanks
Crystal:	not sure i'm ready to think about that yet
Lisa:	just let me know
Lisa:	don't forget to apply for unemployment btw
Crystal:	what's that again?
Lisa:	they'll pay part of your salary if you were laid off through no fault of your own
Crystal:	seriously?
Crystal:	oh wow it says here it can be up to two thirds of your salary
Lisa:	nice
Crystal:	oh but you have to apply for jobs and prove it
Crystal:	i'm not ready to jump into something new yet
Crystal:	i think i want at least a week to recover
Lisa:	well the sooner you apply the sooner they pay you
Lisa:	also no one polices what kind of jobs you apply to
Crystal:	wait, are you thinking what i'm thinking?
Lisa:	maybe...

Crystal: Dear Ringmaster, I'd like to be considered for your rodeo clown position. I have excellent references. Yours Truly, Crystal Hemmingway

Lisa: LOL

Crystal: but isn't that cheating?

Lisa: your employer is legally required to pay for unemployment

Lisa: the money is there already

Crystal: well in that case...

Crystal: this is actually kind of exciting

Crystal: there must be hundreds of jobs that i'm horribly unqualified for

Crystal: and i only have to apply for five a week

Crystal: i wonder how long i could ride this

Crystal: i could just focus on writing for once

Lisa: ☺

Crystal: ok i'm going to go apply for this right now

Crystal: but before i go, can i ask you a favor?

Lisa: sure

Crystal: don't tell mom about my job situation

Lisa: of course

Crystal: i don't want her feeling sorry for me and calling all the time

Lisa: my lips are sealed ☺

Crystal: thanks you're the best

Crystal: ttys

MARGOT'S JOURNAL, SATURDAY JULY 22

I had another walk with Ingrid this morning. Her husband had a stroke, and he lost motor function on the right side of his body. They think he'll get it back with therapy, but poor Ingrid is serving as a full-time caretaker now that he's back home. She's having to make all the meals, do all the housework, and drive him to all his appointments. It's no small feat – he weighs over 200 pounds and she can't be more than 120. He has a wheelchair, but they don't have a car set up to handle that kind of thing. Sometimes it's really hard being alone, but I'm not sure it would be any easier to be in Ingrid's position right now.

Mother's still asking if I can come to the fundraiser this year. I haven't heard back from the girls yet about their holiday plans. I think I'll give them two more weeks, but then I'll just go ahead and book a flight. Mother said I could spend Christmas in Minnesota, so at least I'd have somewhere to go.

I had my weekly call with Crystal today. I asked her how she was doing but she seemed distant or distracted. Work was "fine," David was "fine," she was "fine." She kept giving one-word responses and I was starting to feel like I was prying, so I told her about my week. Then Grace called in the middle and I had to take it, which lasted about 20 minutes. When I called Crystal back I wasn't sure if I should subtract that twenty minutes or add it on, and it was very confusing. But Crystal seemed to want to go at 3 pm as we'd planned, so I hung up. Almost as soon as I did, I realized that I forgot to tell her about the leftover cookies I'm mailing to her. I wanted to just call back like I used to, but I was trying to be respectful of her two-hour limit so I'll have to send an email instead.

This once-a-week, two-hour call feels very restrictive, but I'm going to try it for a couple of weeks and see how it goes. It's going to be awkward when people ask about her and all I can say is that she's "fine," but if this is what she wants, I'll try to respect it.

I hope things slow down again soon for her at work, because she seemed so distracted today. It must be really tough working such long hours, especially since she doesn't get free dinners like Lisa. Maybe I should add some food to her care package. I saw some new vegetarian box mixes at Whole Foods, and I bet she'd enjoy them. And maybe some chocolate, too.

Dr. Jackson had me assist with all of his procedures this week. I really prefer the cleanings to the fillings and crowns; the patients look positively miserable in that chair. The younger hygienists always seem to find a way out of it, so I keep finding myself assisting the doctor. He's good at what he does but I wish he wouldn't try to be such a comedian. His jokes are rather tired and I think our patients might be more relaxed if he wasn't trying so hard.

I always get compliments on my bedside manner (best in class), so I keep telling Dr. Jackson that cleanings are where I do best. Yet each week I seem to be on more procedures, where I'm doing very menial work. If this keeps up, I might have to find another office. I've been doing this for years and I work well on my own; it's frustrating to have to go back to assistant work. I'm going to do my best to pitch in for now, but I'm still going to ask for what I want.

Gratitudes:

1. I am grateful for my health and mobility.
2. I am grateful for my independence.
3. I am grateful for my daughters.

BOOPLE CHAT, THURS JULY 27 4:42 PM

Crystal:	I THINK MOM KNOWS
Lisa:	?
Crystal:	about the layoff
Lisa:	really?
Crystal:	yeah
Crystal:	she sent me a care package, with cookies and stuff
Crystal:	it's not even a minor holiday, so there's no other explanation
Crystal:	oh god, do you think she knows about david, too???
Lisa:	hang on
Lisa:	did it contain tooth-shaped sugar cookies?
Crystal:	yeah
Crystal:	wait, how did you know?
Lisa:	she sent me one too
Lisa:	they're leftovers from the bake sale
Crystal:	what bake sale?

Lisa:	it was for work, and she made like 12 dozen cook-ies
Crystal:	why did she make so many?
Lisa:	long story
Lisa:	anyway, nothing to worry about
Lisa:	and there's no way she'd find out
Lisa:	i haven't told anyone
Crystal:	ok thanks i feel better now

EMAILS, AUGUST 6

From: Crystal Hemmingway <crystalkitty_01@booplemail.com>
To: Office Manager <luxuryliving@moonstoneproperties.com>
Subject: Late rent payment

Dear Ms. Rodriguez,

I'm very sorry to hear about the late rent payment. My co-renter, David Richards, has limited internet access and sent funds to your office on July 17th. I had hoped that they would arrive by now, as he was sending them electronically. I would greatly appreciate it if you could double-check for me, as it was quite a large sum.

In the meantime, I have submitted the second half of our August rent online today. I can certainly pay the late fee, but as it is our first time in three years missing a payment, would it be possible to keep it off the record as a show of good faith?

Thank you for your help.

Yours Truly,
Crystal Hemmingway
Apartment 2212

EMAIL, AUGUST 14

From: Crystal Hemmingway <crystalkitty_01@booplemail.com>
To: Nannies Now! <nannies4hire@nanninesnow.com>
Subject: French-speaking au pair position

Bonjour!

Please accept my attached resume for your French-speaking au pair position. I am passionate about French culture, and enjoy wearing striped shirts and berets. My favorite food is French onion soup. I can speak several words in French, including "le louvre," "croissant," and "au revoir." I have no experience with small children, but I once had a kitten who required daily flea baths.

I have a driver's license and an unmarked white van ready for immediate use.

Thank you for your consideration,
Crystal Hemmingway

EMAIL, AUGUST 25

From: Crystal Hemmingway <crystalkitty_01@booplemail.com>
To: David Richards <darth_david@booplemail.com>
Subject: Funds lost in transit?

Hi David,

Sorry to bother you again, but I've checked with the apartment office several times now, and they still haven't received any funds from you. I'm sure it's just a mix-up, but September rent is coming up soon, so I thought I'd check in again, since I haven't heard from you for a couple of weeks now.

I tried calling your parents but it sounds like they're out of town for the next couple of weeks.

Hope all is well and that you are enjoying your hike.

Best,
Crystal

BOOPLE CHAT, THURS AUG 31, 1:19 PM

Lisa:	good news
Crystal:	!!!!
Lisa:	my department transfer just came through
Crystal:	OMG!! CONGRATS!!!
Lisa:	yeah i'm pretty excited about it

Lisa:	it's a really nice gig, better than i expected
Lisa:	i wish i could tell you about it but all i'm allowed to say is that it's in R&D
Crystal:	top secret, eh?
Lisa:	heh nothing so glamorous
Crystal:	does it have something to do with drones?
Lisa:	no
Crystal:	self-driving cars?
Lisa:	no
Crystal:	cars that transform into robots?
Lisa:	LOL i wish
Lisa:	anyway i've got a few minutes until the desk move
Lisa:	how goes the novel?
Crystal:	going well ☺
Crystal:	got 60 pages or so now
Lisa:	that's great
Lisa:	you still doing a fairy tale thing?
Crystal:	yeah a sort of sequel to rapunzel
Lisa:	cool
Crystal:	i didn't make a lot of progress last week because i binge watched a few seasons of gilmore girls
Crystal:	but since then i cut back to one episode a day
Lisa:	sounds good
Lisa:	did you get to the part
Crystal:	NO SPOILERS
Lisa:	where rory starts dating that
Crystal:	SHUT UP

Lisa:	hot guy?
Crystal:	not funny
Lisa:	you've seen it all before
Crystal:	yeah but i forgot everything
Crystal:	it's all about the joy of rediscovery
Lisa:	aww
Crystal:	plus it keeps me from missing david so much
Lisa:	☹
Crystal:	it's alright, i'm used to it now
Crystal:	anyway tell me more about your new gig
Lisa:	i can't...at least until i get a better idea of what's ok to share
Crystal:	ah right sorry
Crystal:	oh no
Lisa:	what happened?
Crystal:	someone wants to interview me
Lisa:	who?
Crystal:	a nanny agency
Lisa:	but you hate kids
Crystal:	exactly
Crystal:	i thought i explained that in the letter
Crystal:	here i'll forward it to you
Lisa:	hehe you got the unqualified part
Lisa:	but i think you underestimate how desperate they are
Lisa:	nanny agencies like this probably have a huge turnover

Lisa: i bet their major qualification is that the kids come back alive

Crystal: but i even put in the thing about the unmarked white van

Lisa: if you were actually a child molester you probably wouldn't announce that you have an unmarked white van

Crystal: hmm true

Crystal: so what do i do?

Lisa: can you refuse the interview?

Crystal: i think i might get disqualified from the unemployment benefits if i do

Lisa: ok well i think they're looking to hire almost anyone who breathes

Lisa: so your only option might be to say you're super busy

Lisa: like give them fifteen minute windows in which you're available

Lisa: and you might want to breathe really heavily on the phone and speak really slowly, just take forever to answer the questions and they'll probably cut it short

Crystal: ok thanks, you're a lifesaver

Lisa: gotta go, desk moves

Crystal: kk, congrats again ☺

Lisa: thanks ☺

EMAIL, SEPTEMBER 1

From: Crystal Hemmingway <crystalkitty_01@booplemail.com>
To: Office Manager <luxuryliving@moonstoneproperties.com>
Subject: September

Dear Ms. Rodriguez,

Thank you for all of your help searching for the funds from my co-renter, David Richards. I can only assume that they are lost in transit, and I'm sorry for the delay.

I have submitted my full September rent online today. However, until my co-renter returns, are there any discounts that might be available on the lease? I am between jobs at the moment and have actively been interviewing for new positions, but I'd like to stretch my savings as far as possible. We have enjoyed being residents here for the past three years and would hate to have to move.

Thank you for your help.

Yours Truly,
Crystal Hemmingway
Apartment 2212

MARGOT'S JOURNAL, SATURDAY, SEPTEMBER 2

Poor Crystal. Things were worse at her job than I thought. I saw a news story on the internet about how her company, Princesses, Inc., is outsourcing several jobs, and how people were laid off. I asked Crystal about it, and she broke down in tears, poor thing. She was laid off this week, but she didn't know how to tell me. We had a nice long talk about it, and she had a good cry, too. I'm so glad she was able to let it all out. It's really hard to lose your job like that. I've never been laid off, but I've resigned from a few dental offices when things were going downhill. It's hard when the workplace turns into a toxic environment, and you come home feeling icky every day.

I asked Crystal if she has any ideas about what she wants to do next, and she said she's considering taking some time off to work on her novel. She said that she doesn't have a lot of savings, but she might be able to live off it for a little while if she's frugal. I offered to let her move in with me, in case money was an issue, but it sounds like she wants to stay in L.A. with David for now. I wouldn't want her to move back permanently (I do enjoy my independent lifestyle) but I wanted to put it out there just in case.

I think Crystal is going to need more support right now, so I'm going to be sure to check in on her often. I know she has David, but he works during the day, and that's a long time to be alone. It's going to be a big shift for her to go from working every day to job hunting and/or writing. I should probably send her a card to let her know how proud I am, for how well she's handling this whole layoff situation. It's a lot to deal with, but I'm sure the universe has a reason, even if we can't see it yet. Maybe I'll pick up some goodies to send along with the card. Organic chocolate is always a hit.

I'm all set to spend Christmas in Minnesota this year. I'm flying out on the 22nd, so I'll be there to help Mother with any last-minute details for the HHHA fundraiser. That's on the 24th, and I think it'll be good to support Mother on her big day. I'm not sure what Crystal and David are doing this year; it's likely their plans could be affected by Crystal's job situation. Lisa and Bryan will be at his parents, having their "Fontana Christmas." She said I'd be welcome this year, but I'd already booked my ticket to Minnesota. It was probably for the best, because I went to the Fontana Christmas last year, and I felt like the odd one out. They all had all their little in jokes and traditions, which I'm not a part of. On Christmas eve, I happened to mention that I was sensitive to wheat, and Lydia (Bryan's mother) went out to get me gluten-free rolls for the Christmas dinner. It was kind, but no one else even tried a gluten-free one, and they were really bland. When I told Lydia I was sensitive to wheat, I didn't mean that I never ate regular bread, I just meant that I don't eat a lot of it. In the end, I had a whole basket of dry pre-packaged gluten-free rolls sitting in front of me, while I watched everyone else eat the soft, crusty wheat ones from the bakery.

At least she tried.

Work continues to be challenging. Dr. Jackson is upgrading the equipment, starting with the panoramic x-ray machine.

Mom's Perfect Boyfriend

Supposedly, it's going to be simpler and easier than traditional bitewings, but so far, it's been a big hassle. We had a two-hour training to explain how to use it, and all the advantages. I understand that it's more comfortable for patients and there are fewer steps, but right now, all of the steps are new for me. I've done bitewings so many times that I could practically do them in my sleep. This "pano" thing has a lot of steps on the computer, and we have to learn a whole new system. I'm a quick learner, but the instructor sped right through it with a few clicks. I had to ask him to repeat it twice because he talked so quickly, and he mumbled, too. He was drinking one of those energy drinks, and was shaking from all the caffeine. I hope that he's keeping an eye on that, because it's really unhealthy to be hyped up like that all the time.

Gratitudes:
1. I am grateful for Crystal, for sharing with me.
2. I am grateful for Lisa, for inviting me to Christmas at the Fontanas'.
3. I am grateful for my panoramic x-ray instructor, for reminding me to slow down and be patient with others.

BOOPLE CHAT, WEDS SEPT 6, 11:34 AM

Lisa:	omg those sand cat kittens
Crystal:	right????
Lisa:	those eyes!!!
Crystal:	yeah and those markings

49

Lisa:	cutest thing EVER
Crystal:	so what's new at boople
Lisa:	not much
Lisa:	still trying to figure out what i'm doing here
Lisa:	sounds like there's some flexibility in the role
Lisa:	which is a nice way of saying they don't know what the hell to do with me
Crystal:	oh dear
Lisa:	nah it's cool
Lisa:	i've got some ideas on how to fast track my way to a promotion
Crystal:	nice
Crystal:	btw i ended up telling mom about the layoff thing
Crystal:	i wasn't going to but then she saw an article about princesses inc outsourcing and stuff
Lisa:	oh man
Crystal:	yeah
Crystal:	i ended up crying too
Lisa:	aw ☹
Crystal:	i was going to try to stay strong
Crystal:	but then i had to pay the full rent again
Lisa:	still no word from david?
Crystal:	no
Lisa:	aw
Lisa:	you didn't tell mom about you and david yet, right?
Crystal:	no managed to keep that one in, at least
Lisa:	ah ok

Crystal:	so this morning, when i saw the article about outsourcing, i clicked on a link to the princesses inc website
Crystal:	just for fun, i went to "new arrivals" and clicked on the desert palace play set, which was one of my tasks before i got laid off
Crystal:	and i look at the description, since i submitted it right before the layoff meeting
Crystal:	but it's not my description
Crystal:	instead, it says this:
Crystal:	"WHITE PLASTIC TOY"
Lisa:	you're kidding
Crystal:	i wish i was
Lisa:	god that's terrible
Lisa:	it's like describing a granola bar as "FOIL WRAPPED OATS"
Crystal:	pretty much
Lisa:	or a book as "paper wrapped in cardboard"
Crystal:	thanks i got it the first time
Lisa:	heh sorry
Crystal:	anyway i was feeling a little sensitive
Crystal:	and then when mom asked me about my job it didn't take much for it to all come tumbling out
Lisa:	aw
Crystal:	she did that thing where she sounds all sympathetic
Crystal:	but you feel like she's secretly delighting in it

Lisa:	yeah like she's thrilled that she gets to be the shoulder you cry on
Crystal:	exactly
Crystal:	makes me feel manipulated
Lisa:	yeah
Crystal:	i know she's trying to be supportive, but still
Crystal:	she's been calling me every day since, and texting me all these cheerful messages
Crystal:	she even sent me a card with an otter on it saying, "You are otterly amazing!"
Lisa:	oh dear
Crystal:	i don't know why, but it makes me feel even more like a loser
Lisa:	yeah
Lisa:	like it rubs in how un-amazing your life situation is at the moment
Crystal:	yeah
Lisa:	and you know she wants you to say the same kind of thing when she's feeling down
Crystal:	exactly
Crystal:	but i can't because that's not who i am
Lisa:	sure
Crystal:	i know she means well, and it's sweet of her to think of me
Crystal:	but i guess i just wish david was here
Crystal:	because his hugs are the best
Lisa:	yeah, that sucks

Crystal:	although he probably wouldn't be proud of me right now
Crystal:	i was actually doing pretty well limiting my interactions with mom before this week
Crystal:	but now it's even worse than before
Lisa:	well don't be too hard on yourself
Lisa:	if he were here instead of finding himself in the mountains or wherever, you wouldn't be talking to mom so much
Crystal:	TRUE
Lisa:	how's the writing?
Crystal:	slow this week
Crystal:	it's hard to focus when i keep getting texts and stuff
Lisa:	yeah i bet
Crystal:	sorry i'm so cranky
Crystal:	i've only got two months of rent left, so if i don't hear from david soon, i'm pretty much homeless
Crystal:	i've even started looking for some legit jobs, but there's not much out there
Crystal:	at first i thought i could be a barista or something on the side but there's no way i could afford this place on that kind of money
Lisa:	yeah ☹
Lisa:	my offer still stands though
Lisa:	if you see anything that interests you at boople, just say the word

Lisa:	you could even crash with bryan and me until you found a good housing situation
Crystal:	aw thanks, but i think your studio apartment is crowded enough without a third wheel
Lisa:	i'm sure we could manage for a couple of weeks ☺
Crystal:	thanks, i'll keep you posted

CALIFORNIA TECH ARTICLE, SEPTEMBER 13

Boople's Smart Companion Program Incites Ethics Debate

SAN FRANCISCO – Boople's new Smart Companion Program is still in the research phase, but it's already drawing scrutiny from ethics experts. Boople has released little information about the program, but they have claimed that its goal is to produce robots "designed for domestic use." Dr. Adrienne Fisher, professor of AI Ethics at the Massachusetts Institute of Technology, recently stated that Boople's language is "deliberately vague," and "conveniently avoids the ethical implications."

"In his book," Fisher explains, "[Dr. Paul Devereux] claims that the next generation of robots will be androids with the capacity to think, feel, and love." She believes the Smart Companions will meet these criteria, and that "it opens a whole host of ethical consequences." Questions of sovereignty, emancipation, payment for services rendered are "only the tip of the iceberg."

"What happens when a robot is faced with the very prospect of his own humanity, or lack thereof?" she asks. "I hope Dr. Devereux has weighed the potential consequences."

Dr. Devereux and the Boople Smart Companion Team were unavailable for comment. However, the program appears to be proceeding, as a recent Boople inventors' meeting suggests that field tests will begin in the next quarter.

BOOPLE CHAT, TUES SEPT 19, 10:12 AM

Lisa:	i have a title now ☺
Crystal:	ooooh tell me tell me
Crystal:	or is it top secret?
Lisa:	no i can tell you
Lisa:	i'm Community Relations Manager
Crystal:	nice
Crystal:	i especially like the "manager" part
Lisa:	LOL right?
Lisa:	sounds important
Crystal:	so just what does a Community Relations Manager do?
Lisa:	that's top secret ;)
Crystal:	fine don't tell me
Lisa:	aw
Lisa:	it's good though
Crystal:	well it'd better be ;)
Lisa:	so how are things in LA?

Crystal: i've discovered an upside to unemployment

Crystal: i can stay in my pjs until the middle of the afternoon, and i don't have to worry about blow drying my hair anymore

Lisa: nice

Crystal: but seriously this city is stupid expensive

Crystal: october rent is coming up and it's going to wipe out half my bank account

Lisa: have you gotten any money from unemployment yet?

Crystal: yeah, but it's not much

Crystal: i'm not going to starve, but it definitely won't cover david's rent

Lisa: ☹

Crystal: i have a little in savings but that's for emergencies

Crystal: and for the record we aren't there yet

Lisa: you want to crash at our place for a bit?

Lisa: the couch is far more comfortable than it looks

Crystal: aw thanks

Crystal: i've been running through options

Crystal: i thought about selling the prada shoes but it'd probably be too little, too late

Crystal: and i could dig into my emergency fund but that wouldn't last long either

Crystal: maybe i shouldn't have blown off that nanny interview

Lisa: you would've been miserable

Crystal: being broke is probably worse

Crystal:	i really wish david's money would show up
Crystal:	but it's been weeks, and i don't think i can wait anymore
Lisa:	i can't believe he just left you with the rent
Crystal:	yeah he's usually a lot more responsible
Crystal:	he's never had a late payment on his credit cards or anything
Lisa:	yeah bryan is like that too
Crystal:	but still i'm running out of options
Crystal:	i'm starting to seriously consider staying with mom
Lisa:	really?
Crystal:	yeah
Crystal:	she said i could stay with her until i finished the novel
Crystal:	i'd have the place to myself most of the day, since she'd be at work
Crystal:	it'd relieve some of the financial pressure at least and i wouldn't have to spend my time working some menial job
Lisa:	makes sense
Lisa:	but are you sure it's a good idea? i mean this is mom we're talking about here
Crystal:	yeah i'm not fond of the idea of walking on eggshells all the time
Crystal:	because there's no way i can meet all her expectations

Lisa:	sooner or later you'll be labeled a Bad Daughter no matter what
Crystal:	probably
Crystal:	but maybe this time will be different, if i'm there to support her
Crystal:	she hasn't had a meltdown in awhile
Lisa:	not that we know of
Crystal:	hmm true
Crystal:	I'm not thrilled about moving back in with mom
Crystal:	but at least i know how to deal with her
Crystal:	if i take a minimum wage job, i could easily end up with the The Manager From Hell
Lisa:	so "the devil you know..."
Crystal:	exactly
Lisa:	have you talked to mom about it?
Crystal:	only in hypotheticals
Crystal:	i wanted to wait until i'd decided for sure
Crystal:	didn't want to get her all excited and then back out
Lisa:	sure
Crystal:	it'd only be for a month or two hopefully, until i can reach david
Crystal:	ideally i'd be back in my own place before he comes home and he wouldn't even have to know about me crashing with mom
Crystal:	but that might just be wishful thinking
Lisa:	you can't worry about what he thinks
Lisa:	it's mostly his fault you're in this mess

Crystal:	i guess
Lisa:	what would you do with all your stuff?
Crystal:	get a storage unit, probably
Crystal:	most of the furniture is his, and mom has a tv and everything so i wouldn't have to bring much with me
Lisa:	might be hard to keep the david situation secret if you're living with her
Crystal:	yeah i have some ideas for that
Crystal:	it's not ideal but if it's only temporary i should be able to swing it
Crystal:	i don't like lying to her but this whole break/breakup thing is really complicated
Crystal:	and she's already super excited about planning the wedding
Lisa:	yeah ☹
Lisa:	oh hey i meant to tell you
Lisa:	i found a writing contest online that you might be interested in...i'll forward the link
Crystal:	cool thanks
Crystal:	hey lisa
Crystal:	this isn't romance, it's erotic fiction
Lisa:	yeah i know
Lisa:	i thought you could submit that short story you gave me at my bridal shower
Crystal:	velocirapture??? that was a joke
Lisa:	c'mon IT WAS GOOD

Crystal:	it had a couple of moments but i'd be embarrassed to submit it to something like this
Lisa:	they want creativity
Lisa:	it says right there in the rules
Crystal:	yeah they're probably talking about creative sex positions not horny dinosaurs
Lisa:	you could start the next big trend in ero romance
Crystal:	i doubt it
Lisa:	they only want the first ten pages
Lisa:	and you could win $10,000
Lisa:	that's like $1,000 a page
Lisa:	what do you have to lose?
Crystal:	my dignity
Lisa:	use a penname
Lisa:	pleeeeeease?
Crystal:	no
Crystal:	what's it to you, anyway?
Lisa:	i want to live in a world where there are books called "velocirapture" in the romance section!!!
Crystal:	urgggggggggggh
Crystal:	if i say no are you going to enter this behind my back?
Lisa:	that's a great idea
Lisa:	i mean
Lisa:	of course not
Crystal:	alright fine
Crystal:	but only because there's no entry fee
Lisa:	YESSSSSSSSS

Lisa:	i can see the headlines now: "Velocirapture: How Dinosaurs Captured the Hearts and Loins of America"
Crystal:	don't make me regret this
Lisa:	never

EMAIL, SEPTEMBER 20

From: Frank and Debbie Richards <fdrichards_57@boople-mail.com>
To: Crystal Hemmingway <crystalkitty_01@booplemail.com>
Subject: Re: David

Dear Crystal,

Sorry we missed your messages. We took the RV to Yellowstone and decided to go "off the grid" for a few weeks.

We were sorry to hear that David's rent got lost in the mail. We just had a postcard from him. He passed Mt. Hood and is now in the more rural areas of Oregon. His internet access is very limited, but we will pass along your message as soon as we hear from him.

Is there anything we can do to help? How much is his rent payment?

Regards,
Debbie and Frank

EMAIL, SEPTEMBER 20

From: Crystal Hemmingway <crystalkitty_01@booplemail.com>
To: Frank and Debbie Richards <fdrichards_57@booplemail.com>
Subject: Re: David

Dear Debbie and Frank,

Thanks for your note. Hope you had a great time in Yellowstone. I enjoyed the pictures you posted on Facebook, especially those of Debbie and the grizzly cubs. Glad you were able to recover your potato salad before the mama bear arrived.

Thanks for the update on David. Sounds like he'll be out of range for awhile, so please don't worry about the rent. I will cover it myself for now and I can sort it out with David once he returns.

Thanks again for your help.

Best,
Crystal

MARGOT'S JOURNAL, FRIDAY SEPTEMBER 22

My life is about to change. In less than two weeks, my daughter is going to move back in with me! It's only a temporary arrangement (Crystal says it'll be no more than two months), but I think it's going to be a lot of fun.

We talked it over a lot the last few days, and I think this is the best solution. It sounds like David is leaving on a sabbatical soon, so they're going to give up their apartment next month. David is going on an extended camping trip with a friend to contemplate the next steps in his game development career. I think it's a wise choice, considering how depressed he seemed in Hawaii. David and Crystal will do the long-distance thing. Her goal is to finish the first draft of her novel before he gets back.

Crystal is still on unemployment at the moment, and she'd lose that if she got a job at a grocery store or some other minimum-wage position. We ran the numbers, and it makes more sense for her to continue holding out for a job that suits her talents better, and focus on her novel in the meantime.

It's going to be interesting living with her again after all this time, because we've both grown and changed. I'm just glad that I'm able to be there for her at such a challenging time in her life, to help ease the transition to her next job. Crystal seemed to enjoy her work at Princesses, Inc. well enough, but I think she was overworked and underpaid. I'm excited to see where the next chapter in her life will take her, because it feels like there are so many more exciting opportunities available to her than there were before.

It's going to be a bit of a transition, though. I keep quite busy and have a lot of commitments each week. I told Crystal that she doesn't have to worry about rent for now, so hopefully she won't stay long enough for that to become an issue. She'll have some good long hours to write while I'm at work, but I'll probably have to talk to her about splitting up the chores on the weekends. When she visited in the past, I usually played the hostess, but I hope she doesn't expect me to wait on her when we live together. I'm going to make sure that we both pull our weight, but we'll have our fair share of fun, too.

I've gotten so used to my own company; it'll be different having someone around again. I hope she understands that I'm going to need some quiet time to recharge now and then. There will be some advantages too, I imagine. We'll be able to go on walks together, especially down by the beach. We could go to the farmers' market on the weekend, and say hi to Grace and Alice. Maybe Crystal could pitch in with the cooking, and I would finally have time to start a side business. Something fun, maybe. Like baking.

I already had a busy weekend planned, but now Crystal will be moving in, too. I want to do a thorough cleaning before she arrives. It would probably be good to go through the closet too, because Crystal will need some space for her clothes and things. She told me that she's renting a storage unit, but we can't have her living out of a suitcase for two months. I want her to be able to hang up her clothes and put her things in one of the bathroom drawers, so I don't have to see her suitcase sitting out all the time.

Gratitudes:
1. I am grateful for the opportunity to support Crystal during her career transition.
2. I am grateful for my freedom and independence.

3. I am grateful that Crystal does not have a small dog or other pets that could ruin my furniture.

TEXT MESSAGES, SEPTEMBER 24

Mom:	How is your day going?
Crystal:	Fine, just planning for the move.
Mom:	Anything I can do to help?
Crystal:	I've got it, thanks.
Mom:	I'll be here if you need anything!!
Crystal:	Thanks ☺
Mom:	Love you SO MUCH <3
Crystal:	Love you too ☺

TEXT MESSAGES, SEPTEMBER 29

Mom:	Looking forward to the move tomorrow!!!
Crystal:	Yep it's getting close. ☺
Mom:	Any special food/snacks you need?
Crystal:	I'm fine thanks.
Mom:	Yes, I'm sure the non-perishables will survive the trip. We can always go to the grocery the first day if there's anything you're missing.
Crystal:	Thanks, I'm sure what you have will be fine. ☺
Mom:	Ok, I love you! Have a great day!!!
Crystal:	You too ☺

Rapunzel cast a long look back at the palace.

"You'll be back before you know it," said Dame Gothel. "It's just a little hiccup, that's all."

Rapunzel nodded, but she wasn't so sure. Yesterday, she'd been in the midst of planning a royal wedding, but today, the prince was a stranger. Now that some of the numbness had worn off, she longed for an explanation for his sudden change of heart, but Rapunzel wasn't sure she'd ever get one. He didn't owe her anything. He was no longer her William. He was the prince, and she was just a commoner, skulking out of the servants' entrance with little more than the clothes on her back.

"My poor girl," said Dame Gothel, pulling Rapunzel in for a hug. "He still loves you, I'm sure of it."

Rapunzel's eyes prickled with tears. She had been so worried that her mother would be angry, but Dame Gothel had only said, "How could I ever be angry with my daughter?"

"Let's get you home, then," she said, now helping Rapunzel into the hired carriage.

The wooden seat felt cold and rough beneath her skirts, a stark reminder of her upbringing. *This is where I belong,* thought Rapunzel. *I'm no princess.*

The carriage jerked forward and rounded a corner, hiding the castle from view.

Dame Gothel beamed up at Rapunzel. "Everything in the tower is just as you like it," she said. "I've washed and pressed your bed linens, and I had your harp tuned. I found currants at the market so we can make those cookies you love – we'll have so much fun!"

Rapunzel smiled back at her, but her heart wasn't in it. Dame Gothel's enthusiasm should've been comforting, but instead it felt suffocating. Rapunzel was a commoner, and, by all rights, she had no place at the prince's side. And yet, for a few blissful weeks, she had it all. And it was impossible to pretend that things could go back to the way they were. Dame Gothel was right – the currant cookies *had* been Rapunzel's favorite – but that was before she tasted pastries fit for a king.

It will have to be enough, Rapunzel decided. I was happy enough before, so I can be happy here again.

Dame Gothel chatted the whole way home, but Rapunzel barely heard her. When they finally pulled up outside the stone tower, Rapunzel stepped out of the carriage and gazed up at the window where she had once let her hair down for the prince who had stolen her heart.

"It's smaller than I remember," she murmured.

Realizing that it might sound insulting, she glanced at Dame Gothel, but she appeared not to have heard her.

"I'll put on the kettle," Dame Gothel said. "I've got your favorite chamomile tea and wildflower honey."

Chamomile. Her mother always made it the same way, steeped to a shimmering golden color with a spoonful of honey. As a child, Rapunzel had delighted in it, but as she grew older, it seemed sickeningly sweet. She never had the heart to tell Dame Gothel, but when she was at the palace, Rapunzel had taken her tea without honey or sugar, and had grown fond of the complexities of the unsweetened flavor.

Rapunzel would have preferred the tea plain, but she knew the trouble and expense of procuring the tea and honey on her mother's modest income.

"Chamomile sounds lovely," said Rapunzel.

Dame Gothel beamed with pride, and Rapunzel knew she'd answered correctly.

"Welcome home, dear," said Dame Gothel.

BOOPLE CHAT, MON OCT 2 10:13 AM

Crystal:	heya
Lisa:	hey! how's it going?
Crystal:	i'm alright
Crystal:	how are you?
Lisa:	good
Lisa:	i'm managing some community relations ☺
Crystal:	how delightfully...vague
Lisa:	i can't say much now, but hopefully i can before long

Lisa:	if you sign an NDA i might be able to get you into a user test
Crystal:	really? that'd be awesome
Crystal:	wait, it's not for a nose hair trimmer or something, is it?
Lisa:	nope, i think you'll like this one
Crystal:	ok cool
Lisa:	how did it go yesterday?
Crystal:	well most of david's stuff is now in a storage unit in marina del rey
Crystal:	and mine is crammed into mom's apartment
Crystal:	moving was a pain, but at least it's down to unpacking now
Lisa:	☺
Lisa:	how's mom?
Crystal:	oh the usual
Crystal:	she texted me fifteen times already today
Crystal:	more random photos and whatnot
Lisa:	she's excited, then?
Crystal:	yeah
Crystal:	it's really nice of her to let me crash here, so i don't want to complain too much
Crystal:	but i won't get any writing done if i have to keep answering texts every 10 minutes
Lisa:	yeah
Crystal:	i wish i didn't feel like such a failure
Lisa:	aw, what do you mean?
Crystal:	back in july, i was going to set boundaries

Crystal:	talk to mom once a week and all that
Crystal:	and now here i am, living with her
Lisa:	it's for your novel
Crystal:	i know, but i can't shake the feeling that david would disapprove
Lisa:	well he's not here, is he?
Crystal:	no
Crystal:	oh god, do you think he's seeing other girls?
Lisa:	he's been gone for months and this just now occurs to you?
Crystal:	hey easy to say when you're married
Lisa:	sorry
Lisa:	he's still emailing you, right?
Crystal:	sort of
Lisa:	did he say anything about being exclusive?
Crystal:	not in so many words
Lisa:	you might have to ask him, then
Crystal:	because that wouldn't be awkward to ask over email AT ALL
Lisa:	well it's not like you can just call him
Crystal:	TRUE
Lisa:	i've got a meeting in a few minutes
Crystal:	ok
Lisa:	but before i go
Lisa:	don't let david or anyone else make you feel like a failure
Lisa:	it's ok to rely on other people sometimes
Lisa:	that's what mom and i are here for

Crystal:	aw thanks
Crystal:	ttyl then
Lisa:	☺

TEXT MESSAGES, OCTOBER 4

Mom:	Guess who came in for a cleaning today?
Crystal:	Who?
Mom:	Gladys Rickles!!!
Crystal:	?
Mom:	She's a friend of your Grandma's. They used to play bridge back in Northfield.
Crystal:	Ah ok
Mom:	She used to just come to San Diego for the winter but now she's a full-time Californian! Isn't that a crazy coincidence?
Crystal:	Yep ☺
Mom:	How's your Wednesday?
Crystal:	Fine, just working on my novel
Mom:	Sounds like fun!
Crystal:	Yep
Mom:	Ok my lunch break is over, talk to you later!
Mom:	I love you!
Crystal:	Love you too

EMAIL, OCTOBER 8

From: Dr. Thomas Jackson <drjackson@sandiegosmiles.com >

To: Margot Hemmingway <margot@sandiegosmiles.com>
Subject: Prophy Jet training materials

Hi Margot,

Attached are the Prophy Jet training materials. Please review these over the weekend, as we will begin offering this service to clients starting Monday. As a friendly reminder, we'll use traditional polish on patients with porcelain veneers, as the Prophy Jet can damage the glaze.

Keep Smiling,
Dr. Jackson

EMAIL, OCTOBER 8

From: Crystal Hemmingway <crystalkitty_01@booplemail.com>
To: David Richards <darth_david@booplemail.com>
Subject: New apartment

Hi David,

Just wanted to let you know that I gave up the old place. I put your stuff in a storage unit in Marina Del Rey. I've attached the rental agreement to this email. If you show them a photo ID, you should have access to your stuff.

I'm living with a roommate at the moment, but I don't think it'll be a long-term situation, so I'll forward you the address when I'm settled somewhere more permanently.

Hope your hike is going well.

Best,
Crystal

P.S. Sorry to even ask this, but are we still on a break?
P.P.S. Does "break" mean we're still exclusive?
P.P.P.S. Not that I'm interested in anyone else right now...just asking.

EMAIL, OCTOBER 8

From: David Richards <darth_david@booplemail.com>
To: Crystal Hemmingway <crystalkitty_01@booplemail.com>
Subject: Re: New apartment

Hi Crystal,

It's great to hear from you! I just got caught up on all your emails. My internet access has been sporadic at best, so I'm sorry I've been out of touch for so long.

I'm so sorry about the rent money. I called the bank today and it sounds like the transfer never went through. There must've been a mix-up when I tried to send it from Canada.

I went ahead and transferred money directly to your account for August, September, and October rent, plus a little extra for late payments, etc. I included $300 for the storage unit as well. Will that cover it until December?

Again, I'm so sorry about the rent issues. If I'd known it was lost, I would've contacted you sooner.

-David

P.S. Yes I think the best way to describe this is "a break." I don't think that means we're exclusive, but I'm looking inward right now (not dating or seeing anyone).

TEXT MESSAGES, OCTOBER 9

Mom:	If you're still at the grocery store, can you please get me some coconut milk?
Crystal:	what size?
Mom:	The canned one
Crystal:	oh i was looking at refrigerated...hang on
Crystal:	regular or light?
Mom:	Light
Mom:	And organic, if they have it
Crystal:	ok
Mom:	Oh can you also get me some cheddar crackers?
Crystal:	yes
Mom:	And yeast and sea salt and artichoke hearts?
Crystal:	there are 50 different kinds of cheddar crackers
Mom:	I meant duck-shaped ones, they're organic

Mom:	But the cheddar rabbits are good too
Mom:	Probably best to get both
Crystal:	i don't see the ducks or the rabbits
Crystal:	i'm going to call it'll be easier
Mom:	Ok ☺

EMAIL, OCTOBER 11

From: Margot Hemmingway <margot.hemmingway@boople-mail.com>
To: Peggy Hemmingway <phemmingway@hhha.org>
Subject: Re: HHHA Fundraiser Photos

Dear Mother,

Thanks for your note. I'm sorry, but I haven't had time to look for the photos of past San Diego HHHA holiday fundraisers. Dr. Jackson is having us use a new salt water tooth polishing system, and I spent the whole weekend training up on it.

Glad that you were able to book Hettie's daughter as the caterer. Her website seems very professional, and her menu seems to offer many crowd-pleasing choices.

Love,
Margot

BOOPLE CHAT, THURS OCT 12, 3:01 PM

Lisa:	yo yo
Crystal:	sup
Lisa:	did you see my email?
Crystal:	the one with the NDA?
Lisa:	ja
Crystal:	it still doesn't tell me what the project is about
Lisa:	of course not
Lisa:	you have to sign the NDA first
Crystal:	ugggggggggghhhhh
Lisa:	you got something better to do?
Crystal:	than sign away my first-born child?
Lisa:	c'mon it's not that bad
Crystal:	have you read this thing? it's creepily thorough
Lisa:	it's no big deal
Lisa:	everyone at boople signs them
Crystal:	is that supposed to make me feel better?
Lisa:	just sign it so i can finally tell you what i'm working on
Crystal:	ok fine
Crystal:	i'm pretty sure i just signed away the rights to my genetic code
Crystal:	so if crystal clones start popping up all over the boople campus, it'll be on your conscience
Lisa:	:D
Crystal:	so are you going to tell me or what?

Lisa:	oh i have to wait for the NDA to appear in our system
Crystal:	how long does that take?
Lisa:	somewhere between 4 hours and a week
Crystal:	that's a pretty big range
Crystal:	especially for a place like boople
Lisa:	/shrug
Crystal:	so that's it then?
Crystal:	you're just going to leave me hanging
Lisa:	it's my contractual obligation
Crystal:	>_<

MARGOT'S JOURNAL, MONDAY OCTOBER 16

Today was challenging. Dr. Jackson pulled me aside and said that he's going to cut my hours by 40%. That's almost half of my income! He didn't even seem sorry about it, either. He gave me some explanation about diminished insurance pay-outs and decreased appointment times.

We've had plenty of talks about that before. Some of the other hygienists might feel ok dashing off a cleaning in 33 minutes, but I take pride in my work. You need at least 48 minutes, and that's pushing it. I don't even know how they have time to ask "How are you?" in those 33-minute cleanings. In fact, I've watched, and they hold one-sided conversations with patients as they work. The poor people can barely gargle in reply. It's inhumane.

And then there are those fancy new machines Dr. Jackson keeps bringing in. Those have to be expensive, and I gave up my entire weekend to learn how to polish with salt water, because regular old prophy paste wasn't good enough for him anymore. It's all part of his "modern office initiative" but right now, all it seems to do is confuse our regular patients.

Dr. Jackson let me off a couple of hours early, and my head is still reeling. I haven't told Crystal yet. I don't know what I'm going to do. I could continue working there with a 40% pay cut, and it would be more of the same. It's clear that Dr. Jackson doesn't appreciate my talents, and he has no clue how to run a business. In fact, I think I'd do much better running it myself.

Not that I'd want to run a dentists' office.

I can't leave though. I have some savings, but it's for retirement. And at my age, it's not a good idea to gamble with it. We're probably due for a recession soon, and who knows when I'd see that money again.

But on the other hand, I've been working for almost 30 years. Crystal has barely been working three, and she's taking some time off. So don't I deserve the same? I could take off a couple of months at least, and look for a new dental office after that. If I were home, I could really support Crystal. She's seemed pretty depressed lately. She says that she's writing during the day, but she doesn't have that many pages on her novel yet. I bet if I was there to cheer her on, she'd have more motivation.

I could start a side project, too. Maybe a side business? That might be a little too ambitious. But would it really? You read stories all the time about people who get rich from home-based businesses. They just followed their passions. I have lots of those, so I'm sure I could think of something.

What if my business really takes off, and I never have to clean teeth again? I could be an entrepreneur, and be my own boss. No more boring training videos, dental drills, or halitosis. That'd be nice.

I've got some hard thinking to do. I'll use tonight to do some good research, and then I'll be able to make the right decision.

I can just see the look on Dr. Jackson's face when I resign. He won't know what hit him.

Gratitudes:
1. I am grateful for Dr. Jackson, for opening my mind to other opportunities.
2. I am grateful for Crystal, for inspiring me to take time for myself.
3. I am grateful for Sophia, for showing me what kind of hygienist I don't want to be.

BOOPLE CHAT, TUES OCT 17, 8:58 AM

Lisa: mom just sent me a text saying that she's leaving her job to make marshmallows

Lisa:	is this a joke?
Crystal:	no she put in her notice this morning
Crystal:	dr. jackson was going to cut 40% of her hours
Lisa:	oh man
Lisa:	did you tell her she could get unemployment benefits if she stayed?
Crystal:	i tried but she was pretty determined to leave
Crystal:	she was really upset
Crystal:	she said all this stuff about how toxic the work environment is and how they don't appreciate her there
Lisa:	☹
Crystal:	i think some of it is true, and i don't think that office was a good fit for her
Lisa:	when did she hear about losing her hours?
Crystal:	yesterday
Lisa:	she heard yesterday and she resigned today?
Crystal:	yeah she said she knew it was the right thing to do after sleeping on it
Lisa:	for one day
Crystal:	yep
Crystal:	i tried...
Crystal:	you know what she's like when she makes her mind up about something
Lisa:	yeah
Lisa:	so what's this about marshmallows?
Crystal:	she wants a side project
Lisa:	ah ok so she's not expecting to make a profit

Crystal:	eh i think she's hoping it'll be a profitable side project
Lisa:	:/
Crystal:	she said that she wants to sell baked goods at the farmers market
Crystal:	but apparently they already have a bunch of people making cookies and chocolates
Crystal:	so she found an untapped market in marshmallows
Lisa:	has she ever made a marshmallow before?
Crystal:	i didn't want to ask
Lisa:	well she'll figure it out i guess
Crystal:	yeah
Crystal:	i'm not really in a place to criticize her about income
Crystal:	i'm at her mercy in case you hadn't noticed
Lisa:	aw
Crystal:	but i'll keep encouraging her to be practical when i can
Lisa:	sounds good
Lisa:	glad you'll be there to keep her from going off the deep end
Crystal:	oh i think she might already be there
Crystal:	but i probably am too so it's all good
Lisa:	i didn't realize unemployment was contagious
Crystal:	once you get a taste you can never go back bwahahahaha
Lisa:	oh before i forget

Lisa:	your boople NDA came through
Lisa:	so i can finally tell you what i'm working on
Crystal:	TELL ME TELL ME TELL ME
Lisa:	ok check your email
Crystal:	what is this?
Lisa:	it's an application
Crystal:	yeah but for what?
Lisa:	☺
Crystal:	what the hell is a "smart companion"? is that like one of those smart home speaker things?
Lisa:	keep reading
Crystal:	"meals will be compensated"?
Lisa:	keep reading
Crystal:	"run, jump, and play like any other—"
Crystal:	OH MY GOD
Crystal:	lisa are you working on a ROBOT?
Lisa:	technically, i'm in community relations, not design or engineering
Lisa:	but yes ☺
Crystal:	OMG OMG this is SO COOL
Lisa:	haha
Crystal:	so is it like one of those metal dudes with blocky legs or can you make it look like Jude Law in that robot movie? because Jude Law is way hotter
Lisa:	guess you'll just have to apply and see
Crystal:	urrrrggghhhh
Crystal:	i sign away my firstborn to boople and still all the secrecy?

Lisa: well we haven't rolled out the program yet, so we're still finalizing some details

Lisa: it's all very experimental

Crystal: i see

Crystal: so if i ask nicely, there's a chance i can get Jude Law? and he could bring me chocolates and do the dishes and stuff?

Lisa: and here i thought you were going to ask if he'd be your gigolo

Crystal: ick why would you think that?

Lisa: he was a gigolo in that robot movie

Lisa: or were you too busy drooling to pay attention?

Crystal: :P

Crystal: oh wow this application is super long

Crystal: "estimated four hours to complete"?

Lisa: yeah boople likes to have all the info upfront

Crystal: what do they need, my life history?

Lisa: i haven't actually looked at the questions

Lisa: only the dev team gets to see that stuff

Crystal: oooo super secret

Crystal: ok i've gotta get back to writing

Crystal: mom's coming home for lunch and i haven't written anything yet today

Lisa: good luck

Crystal: yeah have fun making ROBOTS

Crystal: i mean community managing ROBOTS

Lisa: ;)

MARGOT'S JOURNAL, THURSDAY OCTOBER 19

It's been an exciting week. I've officially registered my new business, Margot's Mallows. I had several other excellent ideas for the name, including Hallowed Mallows and Margie's Marshies, but Crystal insisted that I keep it simple and sweet. So Margot's Mallows it is.

I drove all over town today to look at commercial kitchens, because you can't sell marshmallows that you make in your home. It turns out that I also need to have a Food Safety Manager Certification, and liability insurance. The manager certification requires an 8-hour training course, and then an exam at the end. I was able to get registered for a class next week, but between the training and the exam it's going to be awhile before I can start cooking. I was hoping to be at the farmers' market a week from Sunday, but that seems unlikely. In the meantime, I'm going to have to look at insurance and get my recipe down.

It's much cheaper to buy ingredients in bulk, but I have to know what I'm going to use first. It would've been easy just to order a gallon of corn syrup and whatnot, but I'd heard about the dangers of it so I've been looking into alternative recipes. It's a good thing, too, because the woman from the farmers' market said they won't allow their vendors to sell foods made with corn syrup and artificial ingredients. She also asked me if I'd make vegan and gluten-free products, which sounded nice, so of course I agreed. That was before I knew that I'd need a certified gluten-free kitchen, which costs an extra $5 an hour, and that vegan marshmallows are much harder to make. Apparently there's a lot of challenges because of the no-gelatin thing.

It can't be too hard though, right? I just need to get to the grocery store and start experimenting in the kitchen. I'm sure I'll find my signature recipes in no time.

I just wish it wasn't all so overwhelming. And expensive. Every time I hear about a $25 per hour commercial kitchen rental fee, or a $100 food safety certification, I remind myself that this is an investment. If Grace can sell soaps at the farmers' market, I can certainly sell marshmallows. Granted, she probably didn't have to go through the same strenuous certification process, but this is a sacrifice I'm making for my customers. Why should people feel left out because they don't eat gluten or animal products? Marshmallows are fun, and everyone should be able to enjoy them.

Gratitudes:
1. I am grateful to finally be a business owner!
2. I am grateful to Crystal for helping me narrow down the names.
3. I am grateful to all of the people who helped me learn about starting a marshmallow business today.

TEXT MESSAGES, OCTOBER 19

Mom:	Are my glasses in there?
Crystal:	reading or regular?
Mom:	Reading
Crystal:	no
Mom:	Not on the bathroom counter?
Crystal:	hang on I'll check
Crystal:	nope
Mom:	Did you see me leave them anywhere?
Crystal:	the kitchen, maybe?
Mom:	I already checked there.
Crystal:	are they on your head?
Mom:	Yes! How did you know?
Crystal:	it's a mystery

BOOPLE CHAT, FRI OCT 20 11:03 AM

Crystal:	i think the universe is mocking me
Lisa:	aw, what do you mean?
Crystal:	i'm a finalist in the ero fiction contest
Lisa:	congrats!!!
Lisa:	i told you velocirapture had potential
Crystal:	no this is terrible
Crystal:	they want a full draft by mid-january...75k words
Lisa:	this is your big chance!
Lisa:	you could get 10 grand and become a published author!

Crystal:	i'd rather not make my debut as a dino fetishist
Lisa:	just use a pseudonym ☺
Lisa:	ero makes good money
Crystal:	nah this is just a distraction
Crystal:	and even if i wanted to, there's no way i could write an ero novel
Crystal:	i'm having a hard enough time writing the rapunzel one
Crystal:	mom is around ALL THE TIME
Crystal:	she interrupts me constantly
Lisa:	so write when she's in the shower
Lisa:	or making marshmallows
Crystal:	A) mom gets ready in like 15 minutes and B) she's talking about having me come with her to the commercial kitchen (she wants an extra pair of hands since they charge by the hour)
Lisa:	just think about the ero contest, ok?
Lisa:	i know it's not your ideal project, but it's still a good opportunity
Lisa:	i bet there are hundreds of authors who'd kill for this
Crystal:	fine, i'll think about it
Lisa:	btw did you get a chance to fill out the smart companion application?
Crystal:	ah not yet
Crystal:	having a hard time finding a spare four hours
Lisa:	well i'd really appreciate it if you could ☺
Crystal:	i started filling it out, but i didn't finish

Crystal: TBH i'm not really comfortable with the robot thing

Crystal: i don't really like the idea of something following me around and trying to make me happy

Lisa: but that's what puppies do

Lisa: everyone loves puppies

Crystal: that's different

Crystal: it's like how the whole smart home thing makes me uncomfortable, too

Crystal: it's not about things spying on me as much as my growing too reliant on it

Crystal: and then eventually i'll have to give it back

Lisa: makes sense

Lisa: but if these trials go well, smart companions will be on the market soon ☺

Crystal: ☺

Crystal: i'm sure it's really cool, i just don't think i'd be a good tester

Crystal: i'd be too scared of it to use it properly

Lisa: well if it's any consolation

Lisa: we'd still love to have your help

Lisa: we want all types of testers, even the reluctant ones

Lisa: so if you change your mind, the application is open for another month ☺

Crystal: ok, thanks

Crystal: did you get your tickets for thanksgiving yet?

Lisa:	yeah bryan finally got the vacation days approved
Crystal:	looking forward to seeing you ☺
Lisa:	same! ☺
Crystal:	kinda going nuts here
Lisa:	aw i bet
Crystal:	mom talks like ALL THE TIME
Crystal:	and even when i'm trying to work she's talking to herself
Crystal:	so i keep thinking she's talking to me, and it's super distracting
Lisa:	☹
Lisa:	have you thought about going to a coffee shop or something?
Crystal:	hmm that could work
Crystal:	but i'd have to order something cheap like tea
Crystal:	funds are kind of an issue
Lisa:	sure
Lisa:	sorry gotta run
Lisa:	i've got the dentist at lunch and then packing for the NYC trip
Lisa:	i'll be out all next week
Crystal:	oh right! have a great time
Crystal:	take some cheesy tourist photos for me
Lisa:	will do
Lisa:	ttyl

TEXT MESSAGES, OCTOBER 21

Mom:	On my way home!
Crystal:	Ok
Mom:	I'm going to drop off this paperwork and then head out to the craft store.
Mom:	Would you like to come with?
Crystal:	Do you need help?
Mom:	Not really.
Mom:	Just deciding on packing materials, and getting some ideas for my farmers' market booth. There are so many choices...it's a bit overwhelming.
Crystal:	Would you like company?
Mom:	You don't need to come
Crystal:	I can be showered and ready in 20 minutes.
Mom:	Great!

TEXT MESSAGES, OCTOBER 23

Mom:	I have a surprise for you!!
Mom:	It's a BOGO coupon for the frozen yogurt place!!!
Mom:	Do you want to go today?
Crystal:	sure
Crystal:	what time?
Mom:	How about 3 p.m.?
Crystal:	sounds good
Mom:	Do you mind if we stop at the craft store on the way? I want to look at ribbons.

Crystal:	ok
Mom:	Although I should probably look at flowers, too...do you mind?
Crystal:	sure
Mom:	You mean you do mind or you don't mind?
Crystal:	i don't mind

TEXT MESSAGES, OCTOBER 24

Mom:	Can you please clean the bathroom today?
Crystal:	sure
Mom:	The rags are in the laundry closet
Crystal:	ok
Mom:	And the all-purpose cleaner is under your sink
Crystal:	ok
Mom:	Actually I need it first to clean the kitchen sink
Mom:	It'll be free in 15 minutes
Crystal:	yeah I was hoping to eat breakfast first
Mom:	I guess 7:30 is a little early for you! Hehe!

CRYSTAL'S JOURNAL, OCTOBER 25

I'm exhausted. I didn't think it was possible to be this tired when I'm still technically unemployed. Mom is around all the time, so I've been staying up late to write my novel. Unfortunately, Mom always seems to have some noisy chores to start before 8 a.m. (vacuuming, blending, sealing boxes with packing tape), so I haven't been getting enough sleep.

Mom's business hasn't even been registered a week, but she's determined to start selling her marshmallows at the farmers' market next Sunday. Most people would take at least a month or two, but she's chomping at the bit. I'm not sure why, exactly, but I suspect it has something to do with Grace. She keeps muttering her name under her breath, almost like it's some sort of curse.

For some strange reason, Mom seems to think that Grace has set some arbitrary standard for farmers' market quality, and Mom is determined not to be shown up. So if Grace has an "artisanal feel" to her stand, we must, too. Mom and I have been driving all over town to get tablecloths, packaging, gift wrap, ribbons, fake flowers that don't look fake, and a bunch of other junk. She's treating it like there's some sort of exam, and someone's going to be judging them on who's more "artisanal."

I hate to break it to you, Mom, but soap and marshmallows are two different things. I tried to gently explain to her that marshmallows aren't more appealing when gift-wrapped in raffia, but she'd have none of it. "We can't just sell them in plain plastic cartons," she said. "They'll look like gas station takeout!"

And so the craft store frenzy continues.

I honestly thought I'd be able to find some time to write while Mom worked on her business stuff, but I've somehow been unwittingly recruited as her assistant. She's so stressed out lately, and then she gets that desperate tone in her voice, "I just need some help here!" She acts like she just needs me to hold down a finger while she gift-wraps a box of marshmallows, but then it's like I'm pulled into the Bermuda Triangle of chores.

Somehow I find myself unloading the dishwasher, making her tea, or running flashcards with her for the food manager's course. And next week she's booked four hours at the commercial kitchen, but she's all hyped up about how it's not going to be enough time. I could tell that she really wanted an extra hand, so I volunteered. It's supposed to be a one-time thing, but I'm worried that it won't be. I don't mind helping her get started, but it seems like she might get used to having me around, and then it'll be hard for her if I'm not. Marshmallows are a sticky business, and from the few test batches I've helped with already, it definitely helps to have an extra set of hands.

I don't think it's unreasonable for Mom to ask me to help. I mean, she is letting me live here, rent-free. And sometimes we even have fun, like when we went out to soft serve on the way home the other day. It's just that I was told that I could have the place to myself for 8+ hours every weekday, while Mom was at work. It was supposed to be a way for me to take some time off and write. But now it's like I'm Mom's unpaid assistant, and I only get to write in the dead of night, when I'm already exhausted.

I want to support her, but if I'd known it was going to be like this, I would've taken some sort of minimum-wage job instead. Because at least then I could clock in and out, and leave my work behind. But lately it's like I'm her full-time help and her full-time therapist, and my writing is getting sidelined. I'm not sure any of my writing is any good right now, but I guess something is better than nothing, right?

I just hope something is salvageable. I don't think I could bear to start over again.

RETURN TO THE TOWER, PAGE 122

The festival was one day away. Rapunzel's week had passed in a flurry of activity, bottling potions, pressing flowers, baking cookies, and practicing her harp. Dame Gothel had a stall at the market each year, and always returned with an empty cart and bulging pockets. In years past, Rapunzel had been content to remain at home while her mother did the selling. This year, however, Dame Gothel insisted that Rapunzel take part.

"We're sure to draw quite the crowd this year," her mother said. Dame Gothel had assigned Rapunzel the role of harpist, to help draw people to their stall. This suited Rapunzel fine, as she was more at ease plucking the harp than wooing potential customers.

Ever since she'd returned from the palace, Dame Gothel had given Rapunzel one project after the next, and she barely had room to breathe. Her mother remained ever cheerful, but Rapunzel had quickly realized that the frenzy was just a ploy to take her mind off the prince. It was nearly working, except now that the festival was almost upon them, it was nearly impossible not to think of him.

Rapunzel knew it was unlikely to run into the prince at the market. He had servants to do his shopping, and his father would never let him roam such crowded streets. If he were recognized, his very life would be at stake. And yet, she couldn't deny that she felt a creeping dread as the festival drew near. The tower was stifling, but she'd left her heart in the capital, and she preferred it stay there. To return now, with her wounds still so fresh...it was daunting, to say the least.

And her mother wasn't helping.

Just this morning, Rapunzel was lying in her bed, thinking of how she'd get ready for market day. She was exhausted after weeks of sewing and baking and bottling and practicing, and she wanted nothing more than to rest up for the big day. But she'd been neglecting herself, and she'd be ashamed to be seen like this among the sophisticated city crowd.

Her hair needed to be washed, dried, and brushed. Her best dress needed mending, and she needed to replace the missing button on her cloak. She had no servants to help her with elaborate hairstyles, but she could braid it well enough on her own. Rapunzel couldn't transform herself into a princess, but at least she would look presentable.

Suddenly, Dame Gothel burst into the room, and before Rapunzel could utter as much as a "Good Morning," her mother had laid out a list of chores a mile long.

"Breakfast is on the table," said her mother. "I'll need you downstairs as soon as you're dressed."

Dame Gothel looked tired, but Rapunzel was tired, too. She simply couldn't bear the thought of another day spent bottling various tonics and following her mother's laundry list of chores. The cart was already full to bursting, and Rapunzel was likely to make the trip buried in handicrafts.

"Sorry, Mother," she said to Dame Gothel.

Her mother paused in the doorway. "Beg your pardon?"

She knew Dame Gothel had heard her. This was simply her way of giving Rapunzel a chance to take it back. Normally, Rapunzel would reconsider. And on an ordinary day, she might relent. But not today. This was her only chance to make herself presentable.

"I can't today," said Rapunzel. She met her mother's gaze. "I already have plans."

Rapunzel had been working for weeks on end. A day off shouldn't have been too much to ask.

Dame Gothel moved to the bed, her face unreadable. She perched lightly on the corner of it, and smoothed her skirts.

"Rapunzel, dear," she said. "You never said you had plans."

Of course she hadn't. She didn't think she'd need to. Rapunzel wasn't a child anymore; her time should've been her own. And yet to Dame Gothel, she was still a little girl, locked in a tower.

"I need to mend my cloak and my best dress," said Rapunzel. At Dame Gothel's inquiring expression, she added, "And wash my hair."

Almost immediately, Rapunzel knew she'd said too much. A shadow passed over Dame Gothel's face, and just for a moment, Rapunzel saw a hint of the anger, hurt, and betrayal that lay just beneath the surface. Dame Gothel might appear a magnanimous and cheerful matron, but Rapunzel knew better. Her mother's perpetual cheerfulness came at a cost, and Rapunzel had been foolish enough to provoke it.

"I-I didn't mean…" stammered Rapunzel.

"I understand," said Dame Gothel, in a threatening tone. "I feed and clothe and shelter you, but today, you simply have *more important* things to do than help your mother."

"I'm sorry—"

"I never should've asked for your help. I can handle it on my own. Of course, I should've known you'd be busy today, *washing your hair.*"

"Mother, please, I—"

"That's perfectly alright," said her mother. "You just stay up here and make yourself pretty. I can handle the rest on my own. I just hope you aren't too ashamed to be seen with your shabby mother."

"That's not what I—" began Rapunzel.

But Dame Gothel had already slammed the door.

Rapunzel sighed. Dame Gothel would now be alone downstairs, taking her anger out on the chores and stewing in her martyrdom. There was only one way to solve this.

"I'll be right down, Mother," she said.

Please, God, let me get through market day without seeing William, she prayed. She could deal with the scorn of anyone but him.

TEXT MESSAGES, NOVEMBER 4

Mom:	HAVE YOU SEEN MY SPARE RAFFIA
Mom:	Sorry got stuck on capitals! Hehe!
Crystal:	i thought you put it in the front closet
Mom:	It's not there.
Crystal:	maybe it's here in the bedroom closet?
Mom:	Can you check?
Crystal:	not here
Mom:	I still have 20 boxes to wrap!!
Crystal:	hang on
Mom:	The craft store closed two hours ago!! I can't debut at the market with only a handful of boxes. People would think I'm unprofessional!

Crystal:	it's here, under the bed
Mom:	Can you bring it here?
Crystal:	yep
Mom:	And if you have a minute, can you help me wrap a few?
Crystal:	yep

MARGOT'S JOURNAL, SUNDAY NOVEMBER 5

Today was my debut at the farmers' market! It was a long day, but I think it went well. We got there with plenty of time to set up, and I think the displays looked quite nice (if I do say so myself). I put out our two types of marshmallows (regular and vegan), and had rustic-looking crates to display them. We also got some lovely daisies and hydrangeas, so everything was white and yellow and pale blue. I had a nice periwinkle table-cloth, and all of the marshmallow boxes were tied up in raffia. Crystal said it reminded her of a countryside picnic, and I have to agree!

A lot of people came by. They didn't say anything about the decorations. (I guess they expect it, but it still would've been nice to hear, as people compliment Grace on her stand all the time.) We did get our first sale! Just one for today, but still, it's a good start. We sold a box of vegan marshmallows to a woman who lives out in Oceanside. She had a sister who eats vegan, and she wanted to make s'mores at a campfire on the beach. She was so nice that I gave her a discount. Hopefully business will spread through word of mouth and we'll get more customers next week!

I was so busy that I didn't have much time to shop the market. Crystal offered to watch the stand so I could pop down to get my organic beets and kale from the place on the corner. I was surprised to see that Grace's booth had moved to the center, and she called me over when she saw me. I hardly recognized the place, because she had redecorated the whole thing. It was all in shades of white. She used to have a more rustic feel, but now it was very modern-looking, which, honestly, was a little off-putting. I rather liked the raffia on her soaps, but she told me that she switched to the white ribbon because the raffia was starting to feel "dated." I don't know where she gets these ideas, but the whole thing felt like some trendy spa shop, not like a farmers' market stall. The whole place was crammed with people, which made it very unapproachable and hard to look.

Grace was supportive when I told her how I was taking a break from my job and was now a vendor at the market. She walked with me to our stall, and promised to buy some marshmallows next week (she was out of cash today). She complimented me on the lovely flowers and couldn't believe they were silk. Before she left, she also invited me and Crystal to the HHHA San Diego Charity Wine Tasting. I guess they're holding it at the zoo this year, since they are the chief beneficiary of the funds. It seems an odd place to have a bunch of adults dressed up and drinking, but I suppose it'll be interesting. I'm quite busy lately, so I didn't promise anything, but I told her I'd check my calendar.

Overall, I think it was a good first day at the farmers' market. Even though we didn't sell as many boxes as I expected, I'm still going to keep my appointment at the commercial kitchen this week. It'll be good to have extra stock on hand, because the holidays are coming up, and I'm sure they'll be flying off the shelves in no time. Who doesn't want s'mores for the holidays?

Gratitudes:
1. I am grateful that I am now an official vendor at the farmers' market.
2. I am grateful for my first customer.
3. I am grateful to have friends like Grace who support me.

EMAIL, NOVEMBER 6

From: Peggy Hemmingway <phemmingway@hhha.org>
To: Margot Hemmingway <margot.hemmingway@boople-mail.com>
Subject: Took a spill

Dear Margot,

How is San Diego? We had an ice storm here last week...took a little spill...fractured my hip ...not sure yet how long the recovery will be...might need surgery.

Rosalie mentioned that Grace found a nice young man recently...Philip from Carlsbad. A lawyer, I believe. Hope you are getting out enough...seems there are plenty of fish in the sea. Sounds like Eric Robertson is getting a divorce for sure now...bet someone nice will snap him up soon.

Grace also mentioned that you were selling treats at the farmers' market and something about taking time off from work. Is all well at the office?

Was wondering if you might be able to help with some of my HHHA holiday fundraiser duties. It's been a rough year for the Northfield gals...passing of several relatives, a mortgage foreclosure, and multiple surgeries...the whole nine yards. I'd just need a hand with some phone calls and whatnot, if you can spare a couple of hours a week.

Heard the HHHA San Diego Charity Wine Tasting is being held at the zoo this year...should be different. Have you bought your tickets yet? Grace always sells out.

Much Love,
Mother

EMAIL, NOVEMBER 6

From: Margot Hemmingway <margot.hemmingway@booplemail.com>
To: Peggy Hemmingway <phemmingway@hhha.org>
Subject: Re: Took a spill

Dear Mother,

I'm so sorry to hear about your hip. I hope you won't have to have surgery, and that the recovery goes swiftly. I'd be happy to help with the HHHA fundraiser. I can make phone calls, do internet research, and assist with whatever else you may need.

Regarding work, Dr. Jackson wanted to cut back my hours by 40%. Things had been going downhill at the office for some time, due to his poor management. I have some money saved up, so it felt like the right time to leave. I'm going to take a break for a few months and focus on my new business, Margot's Mallows. I'm making artisan marshmallows. We just started selling them at the farmers' market, but I hope to expand to health food stores nationwide. Crystal took some pictures of our booth; I'll send them along shortly.

Yes, I have tickets to the HHHA San Diego Charity Wine Tasting. Should be a fun evening.

Hope you get well soon.

Love,
Margot

BOOPLE CHAT, NOV 6 9:38 AM

Crystal:	mom's pulling out her eyelashes again
Lisa:	oh dear

Lisa:	was it the farmers' market?
Crystal:	sort of
Crystal:	it's a lot of things, really
Lisa:	uh oh
Lisa:	i saw the pictures of the booth on facebook
Lisa:	looked nice
Crystal:	yeah she put a lot of work into it
Crystal:	she was going for "rustic chic" but i think she got more "rustic"
Lisa:	sounds about right
Lisa:	why was there a sign that said, "Marshmallows NOT soap"?
Crystal:	oh that
Crystal:	yeah people kept coming by asking what our soap was made out of
Crystal:	apparently the marshmallows resembled soap because mom made them in rectangles
Crystal:	and some people misread "Margot's Mallows" as "Margot's Tallow"
Crystal:	like tallow soap
Lisa:	oh man
Crystal:	yeah i had to make an emergency run to the craft store to get the chalkboard sign too
Lisa:	:/
Crystal:	we stayed up until 1 am the night before tying on the raffia
Crystal:	and then today mom decides that she wants to rip it all off and put on ribbons instead

Lisa:	why?
Crystal:	grace has ribbons
Lisa:	ah
Crystal:	yeah
Crystal:	mom modeled her whole stand after grace's, and then grace went and redesigned hers this week
Crystal:	it's probably just an unfortunate coincidence, but mom keeps talking about it
Lisa:	aw
Lisa:	what's grace like?
Crystal:	willowy, pretty, impeccably dressed
Lisa:	uh oh
Crystal:	from what mom told me, i was expecting her to be some snobby she-devil
Crystal:	but she's not that bad
Crystal:	she seems genuine, but definitely lives the rich housewife life
Lisa:	...without being an actual housewife
Crystal:	exactly
Lisa:	no wonder mom hates her
Crystal:	yeah
Crystal:	she's pretty much the opposite of mom
Lisa:	kind of amazing they're friends
Crystal:	i think it's a result of them both being unnecessarily polite
Crystal:	like one of them probably said, "we should grab coffee sometime" and the other was too polite to let the invite slide

Lisa:	and here they are, one-upping each other at the farmers' market
Crystal:	LOL
Crystal:	i should be more compassionate towards mom
Crystal:	she's been working her butt off all week to get those marshmallows ready
Crystal:	and only one person bought them
Lisa:	aw, really?
Crystal:	yeah
Crystal:	it was a bargain-hunter who came along at the end of the day
Crystal:	she struck up a conversation with mom and mom let her have a box for half price
Lisa:	aw
Crystal:	at least she made a sale
Lisa:	TRUE
Crystal:	i don't know what to do
Crystal:	she works really hard, but i don't think she has a strong business sense
Crystal:	and now she's starting to stress out about money
Lisa:	but it's only been a week
Crystal:	yeah she dropped thousands
Lisa:	how???
Crystal:	she bought a mixer, ingredients, tables for the booth, a course on food safety, the works
Lisa:	ah
Crystal:	so now she's asked me to clip coupons and we're going to focus on making frugal meals

Lisa:	☹
Crystal:	i almost forgot
Crystal:	we're going to this wine tasting now too
Lisa:	but mom doesn't drink
Crystal:	it's an HHHA thing, and grace is hosting it
Lisa:	of course she is :P
Crystal:	so how was NYC?
Lisa:	awesome :D
Lisa:	i had to work a lot but i still managed to squeeze in a couple of shows and some amazing dinners
Crystal:	that's great ☺
Lisa:	yeah i'd love to tell you more but i've got to run to the dentist
Lisa:	ttyl?
Crystal:	sure ☺
Crystal:	hey didn't you go the dentist already a few weeks ago?
Lisa:	oh did i say dentist? i meant eye doctor
Crystal:	ah cool no worries
Crystal:	try not to memorize the eye chart
Lisa:	will do ;)

EMAIL, NOVEMBER 8

From: Boople Smart Companions <no-reply@booplemail.com>
To: Crystal Hemmingway <crystalkitty_01@booplemail.com>
Subject: A Smart Companion awaits…

Hi Crystal!

We noticed that you started your application for a Smart Companion, but haven't yet completed it. We know your time is valuable, so perhaps we can sweeten the deal.

Boople is now offering testers a daily stipend to participate in the Smart Companion trial program. The stipend will depend on the engagement level of the user, but will be no less than $100 per day.

In return, we will only ask for a few 20-minute surveys during your trial.

Thanks for your consideration.
Boople Smart Companion Team

TEXT MESSAGES, NOVEMBER 10

Crystal:	Ready to go?
Mom:	I need a few more minutes.
Crystal:	Where are you?
Mom:	Shoe department
Crystal:	Ok I'm here but I don't see you
Crystal:	Are you by the sale rack?
Mom:	No I'm on one of the benches...a blonde woman is helping me find a mate
Crystal:	You're still talking about shoes, right?
Mom:	Of course! Hehe!

CRYSTAL'S JOURNAL, NOVEMBER 11, 9PM

I should probably be working on my novel right now, but there's no way I can focus. We just got back from the HHHA San Diego Charity Wine Tasting, and, to put it mildly, it didn't go well.

Mom was super nervous about the party, like what she was going to wear and everything. She asked me for some fashion advice, and we even ended up buying her a new dress because none of the ones in her closet "felt right." So after our emergency run to Nordstrom Rack, Mom asked me to help with her makeup. I may have accidentally said something about her having large pores (I was trying to say that liquid foundation worked better on skin with large pores), and I tried to backpedal as soon as I said it. I thought it was ok, but more on that later.

Anyway I had to get ready in about 20 minutes, so my party face and hair wasn't the greatest, but it was ok at least. I had some really cute (and sexy) party dresses but I chose to go with something more conservative. Mom was already feeling unsure of herself, and I knew that if I wore something flashy, it'd only make her feel worse. So I went for the retro vibe, and added some low-heeled sandals as well (the Prada sandals remained safely in the closet, away from Mom's judgement).

Mom actually looked quite nice in her dress and with her makeup (and I'm not just saying that because I helped). She wanted to get a quick picture so I suggested that we take one outside, since she has this cool string of lanterns in her back-yard. We took a couple together but I also got some of just her, and a couple of them turned out really well. Like, with a couple of filters it actually looks semi-professional. I think we just got lucky, since the lighting was really great, but it was nice to see Mom looking so happy and pretty. I think it also has something to do with wearing foundation and stuff instead of just eye makeup, but I didn't want to call it out since she's "just not a foundation kind of person" (her words).

So getting to the zoo was a bit of an ordeal, and Mom already had a blister by the time we arrived at the gates. She tried to put on a brave face, but I gave her a band-aid from my purse, since I always carry them. But when we got to the party, it was this huge extravaganza, with colored lights and aerial ac-robats on silks and trendy music. Everyone there looked to be at least 50, and so I was really glad that I didn't wear a sexy dress, because getting ogled by guys my dad's age would've been super awkward. Mom had this creepy smile plastered on her face, and I'm pretty sure she was trying really hard not to be jealous of Grace, and failing miserably.

Then all these waiters came around and offered us like a million glasses of wine, and Mom and I had to refuse every sin-gle one. Mom doesn't drink and I'm not much for it (and I didn't exactly feel like it with her already on edge). A bunch of random people from the HHHA came up to us, and Mom kept introduc-ing me as a novelist, which was super awkward, because I ha-ven't even finished a book.

When it got late, I wanted to call it a night, but Mom insisted on finding Grace to congratulate her on the party. I knew this was a bad idea, but I couldn't stop her, so pretty soon we were standing in front of Grace, who had this guy on her arm. He was incredibly handsome (for a guy in his 50's) and she kissed him right then. Apparently his name is Philip, and he's some sort of lawyer. Mom looked like she wanted to punch Grace in the face (that is, grinning from ear to ear with her false creepy smile), and then some other guy came over to talk to Grace, and I thought we were finally saved.

But then Mom was completely frozen in place. The guy turned, and he looked around 60, with some leggy blonde around my age hanging off his arm. He looked vaguely familiar, and I feel like I should've recognize him from somewhere.

"Margie!" he said, and gave Mom a huge hug.

And then it hit me. I'd seen him on Facebook, in a group photo on Mom's timeline. It was James, the guy who broke her heart so badly that she had to crash my "romantic" Hawaiian vacation.

By this point, Mom was shaking, so I made a hasty excuse about not feeling well and pulled her to a remote corner of the party, back behind the drinks stand.

We plopped down on a bench. Tears were streaming down Mom's face. Her mascara was streaked, making little lines on her foundation, so I handed her a tissue. She blew her nose and blotted the tears, but the streaks were still there.

For the first time today, Mom was completely silent. So I gave her a hug, and then put a hand on her shoulder. I wasn't sure where to start, or what she was going through, so I just sat there with her.

And then it all started tumbling out. How Grace has everything, and how Mom has had to struggle for all these years, on her own. How everyone around her seems to be effortlessly rich, and how Mom has to fight for every nickel and dime. How James dumped her for a girl less than half his age, and how that makes it nearly impossible to find anyone once you're over 50 and divorced. How everyone in San Diego is thin and beautiful, and how Mom can't compete, no matter how hard she tries.

I tried my best to reassure her. She told me that she's feeling unappreciated and that no one needs her, so said that I appreciate her and need her. I think she knew that there was truth to it, but it was hard to see her like this, at such a low. The way she talked, sometimes it seems like she feels invisible, like no one cares. I didn't know what to say, because I do care, but I know that I can't fill the gaping void that's been eating away at her for a decade. No matter how much I reassure her, what she really needs is a romantic companion.

She started to wind down, and then she made some comment about her "large pores" and how awful she looked. I tried not to take it personally, because it's the same kind of thing that happens every time. It doesn't matter that I've tried desperately to say the right thing all night. She only seems to hear the one vaguely negative thing that accidentally escapes, and now she'll probably be staring at her face for hours, obsessing over her "large pores." So I handed her another tissue and told her that she still looked nice, and offered to drive us home.

Now we're back, and Mom is asleep. I feel sorry for her, and honestly, if I'd known James would be there, I probably would've discouraged her from going. But it has been several months, and I guess she can't hide from him forever. Whatever happened between them is their business, but she always insisted they were just friends, and maybe she can get back to that someday. Maybe the best cure for a broken heart is a new love.

Sometimes I wish I could just conjure up a guy for Mom. It seems like it would solve everything. I mean, what she really wants is someone to agree with her all the time, and give her unconditional, non-judgmental love. Kind of like a dog.

Except a dog is not the same as a romantic companion.

No, Mom needs someone who will talk back, so she feels heard. She wants someone to listen, but also to offer advice. That's probably why she calls Lisa and me all the time. And why I'm in this whole mess with David in the first place.

If Mom found a guy to take care of her, then she wouldn't need to lean on me and Lisa so much, and I could have my independence back. I don't think a guy like that exists, though.

Hmmm.

BOOPLE SMART COMPANION ONLINE APPLICATION, PAGE 4 OF 93

Q: What is your favorite movie?
A: Must Love Dogs.

Q: What is your favorite food?
A: Chocolate.

Q: Would you like your companion to:
_X_ Emulate a human
___ Look and act like a machine

Q: I am primarily looking for a companion to:
___ Be a servant (maid, cook, errand person)
_X_ Be a friend or confidant

Q: Describe your ideal companion's appearance.
A: A cross between Robert Redford and Pierce Brosnan, around 55 years of age.

Q: Describe your ideal day.
A: I'd wake up early, with the sunrise. I'd have a cup of tea and then do 30 minutes of yoga. Then I'd go for a walk outside, and make oatmeal for breakfast. I'd spend the morning out and about, going to the grocery store or farmers' market, and then to coffee with a friend or my daughters. I'd make lunch at home, and eat it outside. I'd clean up the dishes and then go out again, probably shopping for clothes or books. Then I'd come home and bake chocolate chip cookies, and I'd eat them warm with milk. I'd eat dinner out at a healthy restaurant, and go for a walk afterwards. Then I'd catch a movie. Once I got home, I'd relax in a hot, candle-lit bath, and journal before bed.

Q: What behaviors do you look for in a companion?

A:

- Good listener
- Liberal with compliments
- Constantly tells me: 1) he appreciates me, 2) he's proud of me, and 3) I am beautiful
- Very handsome
- Healthy
- Active
- Likes the outdoors
- Intelligent
- Compassionate
- Spiritually open-minded (mainly New Age views)
- Enjoys movies
- Loves to travel
- A gentleman (holds doors, offers to drive, etc.)
- Gets along with my parents
- Kind to my daughters
- Patient
- Enjoys eating food (especially dessert)
- Dresses well
- Has a nice car (ideally red)
- Is well-off
- Has a respectable but interesting profession
- Drives a motorcycle
- Helps with chores without being asked
- Tidy/neat
- Puts the needs of others before his own

- Makes me his #1 priority
- Loves children
- Non-judgmental

Q: What type of activities would you like your companion to perform?

A:

- Watch movies together
- Go shopping with me
- Help with chores
- Cook a meal together
- Listen supportively (agree with everything and restate it in slightly different words to show we're on the same page)
- Drive me places in a nice car
- Bring me flowers and other gifts randomly
- Take me on a motorcycle ride
- Man the farmers' market booth with me
- Hold witty conversations with my family and friends
- Travel to new and exciting places
- Snuggle with me
- Light romantic overtures (not past first base)
- Always thinking about how to make me happy

Q: How would you like your companion to address you?

A: Ms. Hemmingway to start. With greater familiarity, I would prefer to be called Margot. If the relationship progresses, acceptable pet names include "beautiful" and "my queen" (on special occasions).

CRYSTAL'S JOURNAL, NOVEMBER 12, 1:30 AM

I just submitted an application to the Boople Smart Companion project on Mom's behalf! With any luck, she'll be selected, and they'll build her a perfect robot boyfriend who falls in love with her at first sight and solves all her problems.

Technology is awesome.

I am a genius.

CRYSTAL'S JOURNAL, NOVEMBER 12, 2 AM

I am an idiot.

What if they pick her? What if she finds out that I'm the one who sent the application? What if she READS THE APPLICATION??

They can't really make robots. I bet it's just a glorified shopping assistant. Lisa used to have one of those, and every time we asked it for the weather report, it tried to order goat cheese.

They probably won't pick her. I mean, worst case scenario: they send her some kind of creepy sex robot, and she finds out that It was my idea. Sure, we'd both be scarred for life, but it's the thought that counts, right?

I am a terrible daughter.

I need to stop thinking about this.

EMAIL, NOVEMBER 12

From: Seahorse Booksellers <info@seahorsebooks.com>
To: Margot Hemmingway <margot.hemmingway@boople-mail.com>
Subject: Shipment confirmation for Order #0003489721

The following items have now been shipped:
- Soulmates now! 10 Steps to Finding Your Twin Flame, by Zoey Chamberlain
- 50 over 50: Simple Ways to Go From Frumpy to Foxy, by Joanne Sullivan
- The Single Lady's Guide to Entrepreneurship, by Claire Reynolds
- Sail Away: A Revolutionary Approach to Releasing Toxic Feelings, by Dane McMasters

Please <u>click here</u> to track your items.

The following items are still in process and will ship separately:
- *Steamed Buns: A Paradise Bakery Romance,* by Athena Dale

Thank you for choosing Seahorse Booksellers, an independent bookseller.

BOOPLE CHAT, NOV 13 3:42 PM

Crystal:	HALP
Lisa:	??
Crystal:	mom suddenly decided it's time to tell the universe she wants a guy
Crystal:	which means she wants to change everything RIGHT NOW
Crystal:	yesterday she went through her closet and got rid of half her clothes
Crystal:	and today we feng shui'd the entire apartment
Lisa:	oh dear
Lisa:	because of the party?
Crystal:	seems like it
Lisa:	did she at least get rid of those fuzzy jackets?
Crystal:	nope those stayed
Crystal:	she read an article online about how you should only wear clothes you love, because they make you feel confident and confidence is sexy
Lisa:	let me guess
Lisa:	this article was written by woman?
Crystal:	yeah
Crystal:	someone named joanne sullivan
Crystal:	i guess she's big with the boomer crowd
Crystal:	how's work?
Lisa:	good
Lisa:	the devs said we got over a dozen applications this week

Crystal: any good ones? ☺
Lisa: i dunno, i don't get to see any of that stuff
Lisa: did you apply?
Crystal: you'll just have to wait and see ☺
Lisa: thought you might like the stipend ;)
Crystal: hey i don't even know if i'll get accepted
Lisa: you probably have a good shot
Lisa: it might depend on what you asked for though, since they're looking for certain kinds of testers
Crystal: ah ok
Lisa: mom sent me a picture of her new pants
Crystal: yeah we went shopping this morning
Crystal: she was determined to buy a pair of faux leather pants
Crystal: and then she broke down in tears because all of them seemed to make her thighs look big
Crystal: i tried to gently imply that stretchy, shiny pants aren't the best for pear shapes but that seemed to make it worse
Crystal: and then she kept making comments about how she "just wanted something fun" and how she "needs to break out of her box" and wear more sexy clothes
Crystal: so in the end we chose the best ones we could find
Crystal: and i had to spend the entire ride home reassuring her that they were a good purchase

Lisa:	was she doing that thing where she's challenging you to disagree?
Lisa:	and if you do, she'll get really mad?
Crystal:	yeah
Crystal:	i don't like lying about these things, but she didn't give me much of a choice
Crystal:	i tried to steer her towards a pair that were on sale at least
Crystal:	since she's still stressing about money
Lisa:	aw
Lisa:	well if it makes you feel any better
Lisa:	she probably would've bought them with or without you
Lisa:	so don't feel too bad about it
Crystal:	thanks
Crystal:	she asks me for fashion advice, and i want to help
Crystal:	but when it comes to things like this, she doesn't want to listen
Crystal:	i was still feeling guilty though so i offered to make her a website
Lisa:	for the marshmallow business?
Crystal:	yeah
Crystal:	i was hoping it would cheer her up
Crystal:	i just roughed something out using a template, but she was super excited
Crystal:	i happened to get a nice picture of her before the zoo party thing, so i used that on the "about" page

Crystal: but she really needs to get some good pictures of her food, because it looks pretty amateurish with the farmers' market snapshots

Lisa: well it's a start at least

Lisa: glad she liked it

Crystal: yeah i managed to keep her from sending it out to her family for a week

Crystal: i'm going to take some more photos at the next farmers' market

Crystal: won't be professional but hopefully better than what's there now

Lisa: ☺

Crystal: gotta go, she wants to go shoe shopping

Crystal: for "sexy" shoes

Lisa: good luck

Crystal: thanks, i'll need it :/

TEXT MESSAGES, NOVEMBER 14

Mom: Can you add smudge spray to the Amazon cart?

Crystal: I thought smudging was "clearing" a space with smoke from a burning herb thing...?

Mom: Yes, but that sets off the fire alarm, so that's why they invented smudge spray. ☺

Crystal: Does it have the same properties?

Mom: Spiritually, yes.

Crystal: The only one on Amazon is $45 for 4 ounces

Mom: Is it Heaven on Earth brand?

Crystal:	yeah
Mom:	That's the one!
Crystal:	ok, added
Mom:	Thanks!

EMAIL, NOVEMBER 15

From: Boople Smart Companions <no-reply@booplemail.com>
To: Margot Hemmingway <crystalkitty_01@booplemail.com>
Subject: Ready to meet your Smart Companion?

Hi Margot!

Congratulations on being approved for the Boople Smart Companion trial program. By now, you should have received several emails with the introductory materials and waivers. We think you're going to love our Smart Companion as much as we do, and we have personalized meet-and-greet appointments available as soon as Friday, November 17.

Please complete the waivers by using the links below. After that, look out for our meet-and-greet RSVP.

Welcome to the future!
Boople Smart Companion Team

CRYSTAL'S JOURNAL, NOVEMBER 16

I did it. I'm officially signed up for a meet-and-greet with this "smart companion." Technically, it's in Mom's name. I filled out the application for her, because I knew she'd never consider it herself. I hate the secrecy, but I really have her best interests in mind. She says that she wants a soulmate, but honestly, her expectations are way too high. So why not try out a guy who's made-to-order?

I know that this is a bit of a risk. He could be completely robotic and obvious and terrible. Mom might not even like him in the first place. Or if she actually does start falling for him, what happens then? There isn't exactly a romantic future. I mean, once they're officially released he could probably be a platonic companion, but he's not exactly the same as a warm-blooded man.

But honestly, I'm not sure that matters to Mom right now. She's truly, desperately in need of a companion. Preferably one who isn't her daughter.

Ok, I realize that this isn't entirely selfless. I've had almost no time to myself when she's awake, and all these late nights working on my novel might be impairing my judgement. But seriously, is it really that bad to ask for a few hours' reprieve? I'm not looking for a babysitter, exactly, just someone to entertain her for awhile. If he can distract her for even an afternoon, this would all be worth it. Mom would never even have to know about the robot thing. Just have a nice date with a nice guy, right?

Except I'm not sure how this whole "date" thing is going to work. Boople told me to go to some dog park near the zoo. But we don't have a dog, and it would seem weird for me to just randomly borrow one for a day, right? So I went online and luckily they're having some volunteer tree planting event at the same park, and they needed some extra hands. Mom was a little surprised when I told her that I wanted to go, but I made some excuse about wanting to get out of the house and connect with the community, and she didn't seem to suspect anything.

So tomorrow we're getting up early (because apparently volunteers aren't allowed to sleep in) and we'll go down to the park to do the tree planting. The volunteer shift will wind down around the time of the Boople meet-and-greet, but they were pretty vague on the instructions. I'm not sure what to expect, but I'm hoping that it goes smoothly. Because there's no way I'm calling to ask Lisa for help. I'm pretty sure it's some violation of Boople rules to apply for a companion for someone else, and it's probably not the kind of thing Lisa would support in the first place. I really didn't intend to keep secrets from her, but she was the one who kept pressuring me to apply. And I honestly think Mom will be a much better test case, since she's actually looking for a companion.

Here's hoping this all goes smoothly.

MARGOT'S JOURNAL, FRIDAY, NOVEMBER 17

We had a nice outing today at the park. Crystal wanted to volunteer at a tree planting, and it was all very last-minute. It was unusual for her, but I wanted to support her interest in community service, so I switched my walk with Ingrid to clear the morning.

We had to get up quite early (6:30 a.m.), which is about an hour before I normally wake up, and almost the middle of the night for Crystal. She practically jumped out of bed this morning. I'm not sure why she was so excited about a tree planting, especially when she's shown no interest in these types of events before. Maybe it has something to do with her novel?

The tree planting was inside a dog park in the Balboa Park area. It was a bit complicated to find the right place, but since it was so early, we didn't run into much traffic and there was plenty of parking.

The tree planting was poorly organized, but we managed. There weren't enough gloves to go around, which was a bit disappointing, because I had considered bringing my own. Crystal gave up on the digging when she started to get blisters about an hour in, so I ended up putting in most of the grunt work. I thought she'd be more excited about the trees, with the way she leapt out of bed, but she seemed distracted. She was talking about going for a walk later, and must've mentioned lunch every fifteen minutes.

Around the middle of our shift, Crystal wandered off to the snack station, and left me on my own to finish the third tree. Just as I was setting it in, a plastic ball came flying out of nowhere, and hit me squarely in the bottom. It stung a bit, and when I saw that it was a dog toy, I wasn't surprised. We were in a dog park, after all. One of the dog owners must have had poor aim and hit me, even though we were in a special roped-off section. I picked up the ball to return it and saw a Pomeranian running towards me, trailing a leash behind it. The dog was yapping like crazy and ran in circles around me, binding my legs together.

I was starting to get quite frustrated with the dog at this point, as the owners should really keep a better eye on their pets. But just then, a very handsome man appeared, and he apologized profusely. There are a lot of good-looking men in San Diego, but this one was a real looker. He had blue eyes and dark hair, and almost reminded me a bit of Pierce Brosnan, with maybe a little Robert Redford mixed in. He looked to be about my age, too.

He seemed very nice and was quite polite as he was unwinding the leash – he had a gentle touch and freed me in no time. Then he was off again, chasing after that overexcited little dog.

He probably had a wife or a girlfriend to get back to. The good ones always seem to be taken, unfortunately. I know that the universe will bring me a man when the time is right, but it would've been nice if he'd at least asked my name. It's hard to stay hopeful when all my online dates have been with average-looking men. I don't think I have unreasonable expectations, but men seem very hung up on having lots of sex, so I don't think it's too much to ask to be physically attracted to them. I used to want there to be a "spark," but now I just want someone halfway decent. As long as they're nice, of course. And know how to treat a lady.

Anyway, we finished planting our trees early, but Crystal felt obligated to work the full shift. So it was more work for me, and Crystal provided some light assistance while we planted another pair of trees. When our shift was over, we took a very slow walk through the park. (Crystal was really dragging her feet for some reason, and kept checking her phone.) The lunch options were fairly expensive nearby, so we drove to Native Foods instead.

Crystal seemed down, so we stopped for frozen yogurt on the way home, which cheered her up a bit. When we got home, I put her to work helping me with the website, since there were some things I needed her help with. Being busy is a great way to pull yourself out of a slump, and I think it did the trick for Crystal. I was exhausted from all that digging, but I had to make some phone calls and do some research on DJs for Mother's HHHA fundraiser. After that, we ate dinner and watched a movie, so it was a full day.

It's a good thing that I have more time to spend with Crystal right now. She seems more moody lately, and can get quiet and withdrawn. I think volunteering is probably good for her, but we might need to find some activities that are more suited to her skills. I think I saw something in my HHHA newsletter about someone who needed tech help volunteers... she'd probably enjoy that more. Or maybe the cat shelter; she's always talking about how she wants to adopt one.

The farmers' market is coming up on Sunday, and Crystal and I will be manning the stand again. We have some prep work to do tomorrow. I still have some marshmallows packaged and ready to go, but we need to make some updates to our décor and print out the flyers. It feels like I spend hours on the business every day, but there's always so much left to do. I hired a company to design my business cards, and they have some nice mockups so far. It would've been nice to have the cards for tomorrow, but these things take time, and I want to get the logo right. Eventually, I'll use it on the marshmallow labels and on a pretty banner for our booth as well. So we need something high-res, not some bitty clip art.

All of this costs money, and it's hard watching it fly out the window so quickly. I keep reminding myself that this is an investment – not just in the business, but in myself. I don't want to limit myself by thinking too small. I'm working to manifest a successful business – the kind of company whose artisan goods you can find in Whole Foods. It's only a matter of time, really. I just have to roll up my sleeves and put in a little elbow grease. The universe will provide.

Gratitudes:
1. I am grateful for Crystal's desire to connect with her community.

2. I am grateful for DJ Dane, who owns Mother's favorite Christmas album (the Do-Re-Mi Children's Choir), and can surprise her with it at the HHHA fundraiser.
3. I am grateful for the man in the park, who had such a handsome smile and reminded me not to give up hope.

CRYSTAL'S JOURNAL, NOVEMBER 17

I only have a few minutes to write, because it's already 9:30 p.m. and I haven't gotten any work done on my novel today (I was with Mom all day and she needed help with her website).

But I did want to mention that my Smart Companion stood me up. There wasn't a single message from Boople the entire day. I looked up and down that dog park, and there was no sign of anyone from Boople. No robots to be found. They didn't even give me a phone number. I woke up at the crack of dawn and pretended to be excited about a freaking tree planting, and for what? NOTHING.

Thanks, Boople.

TEXT MESSAGES, NOVEMBER 18

Mom: Crystal, the website is down!!!!
Crystal: What are you seeing?
Mom: It says the domain is for sale!!!

Mom:	Someone else could steal margotsmallows.com from us!!!
Crystal:	It looks fine on my phone
Mom:	That's so weird!
Crystal:	Did you try reloading it?
Mom:	It's still down!!!
Crystal:	Did you double-check the address?
Mom:	Oh my goodness! I was going to margotswallows.com!!!
Mom:	Can we buy it too and have it send people to the right website?
Crystal:	I don't think you want to be associated with that address...
Mom:	Why not?
Crystal:	umm...

MARGOT'S JOURNAL, SUNDAY NOVEMBER 19

You would not believe what happened at the farmers' market today! Crystal and I were there, manning the stand, when I heard a dog barking. The dog ran right up to me, trailing its leash, and it looked just like the Pomeranian from the dog park on Friday. Well, wouldn't you know it but then that handsome guy from the dog park runs over and scoops up the dog! Turns out the dog's name is Pickle, and she's not his – he's dog sitting for the weekend. How sweet is that?

He recognized me right away, and said, "You're that lovely woman from the dog park!" I think I must've turned beet red, because people usually say "that sweater is pretty" or "you look cute today," but it's rare to have such a handsome guy call me "lovely." I tried to focus on treating him like any customer, so I wouldn't make a fool of myself. I offered him a marshmallow sample, and he said they were "very gooey and delicious." And then he bought two boxes right then and there, one for him and one for his parents. I guess that his parents live in Northern California, and he is close to them.

I thought he was going to head on at that point, but then he was actually a bit chatty. I told him about how I'd left my job as a hygienist recently to start my marshmallow business. He asked me good questions, like why I chose marshmallows and what it was like to sell at the market. He also talked to Crystal a bit, but then she hurried off to get a snack. (I don't know why she didn't want to eat the granola bar she brought, but sometimes she's like that.)

So his name is Adam, and he's a screenwriter. He wasn't allowed to say too much about his work, but he primarily works on films for one of the big Hollywood studios. I had no idea people like that lived in San Diego. I thought they were mostly in Los Angeles.

Then he got a call and said he'd have to go, and I thought that would be the end of it. But then he got out a business card, wrote something on the back, and handed it to me. As he was leaving, I turned it over and it said one word: "Coffee?" And he'd written his phone number below it! I couldn't believe it! I also noticed that he didn't have a wedding ring, but I was sure someone with such stunning blue eyes would at least have a girlfriend. Maybe he does have a girlfriend. Perhaps the girl who owns the dog? You never know with coffee; maybe he just wants to meet as friends.

Crystal thinks it sounds like a date, and that I should definitely go. I'm so nervous! It's been so long since I've been on a date! I told myself that I would sleep on it, and call him tomorrow. I don't want to seem too desperate.

I can't believe that he wants to go to coffee!

Gratitudes:

1. I am grateful for Adam, for remembering me from the dog park and talking with me.
2. I am grateful for having a (potential) coffee date!
3. I am grateful for marshmallows, which are helping me meet interesting people at the farmers' market.

CRYSTAL'S JOURNAL, NOVEMBER 19

OH MY GOD. It's him. The guy from the farmer's market, Adam. He's the Smart Companion.

At first, I thought it was a really strange coincidence. But then Mom said something about him looking like a cross between Pierce Brosnan and Robert Redford. And I was like, "OMG he totally is," which seemed a little suspicious. And then I got an email from Boople later that afternoon, with a five-question survey about the Smart Companion introduction. And right there, on the survey form, was Adam's handsome mug.

It shouldn't be possible for him to look that realistic. I thought he'd be kind of metallic, or plastic-looking. Like creepily perfect. But I was looking at his face, and the dude had freckles. Stubble. A subtly receding hairline. He looked freaking REAL.

And now Mom keeps giggling every time she thinks about him, which is like every two seconds. If she goes on this coffee date with him, we may reach the point of no return.

What if she falls in love with him?

When she finds out the truth about him, will she blame me? Will I have to be the one to tell her???

If he breaks her heart, it'll probably be worse than the James thing.

And why did they have to make him so handsome? Now Mom's going to have astronomical standards for attractiveness. I might've doomed her to a life of spinsterhood.

What the hell am I going to do??????????

BOOPLE CHAT, NOV 20 1:23 PM

Lisa:	what's this about a coffee date?
Crystal:	mom's going on one
Lisa:	yeah i got that much
Lisa:	who's the dude?
Crystal:	just some guy she met at the farmers' market
Lisa:	ah ok
Lisa:	did you meet him too then?

Crystal:	yeah he seems nice
Crystal:	90% sure he's not a creeper
Lisa:	cool
Lisa:	you think he has potential?
Crystal:	not sure yet
Crystal:	there's still a small chance it's just a friend date
Lisa:	ah
Crystal:	yeah but mom's seriously crushing
Crystal:	she was so distracted that she mixed up the salt and the sugar in her latest batch of marshmallows
Lisa:	wow
Lisa:	not much you can do there then
Crystal:	btw i have some news
Lisa:	tell me tell me
Crystal:	you know how grace has a handmade goats' milk soap stand at the farmers' market?
Lisa:	yep
Crystal:	well i was waiting in line for my pierogis
Crystal:	and the pierogi stall was on the back side of grace's booth
Crystal:	there was this cardboard shipping box sticking out from under one of her tables, and it had some writing on it, in both chinese and english
Crystal:	turns out grace's soaps aren't so handmade
Crystal:	she's buying them in bulk from china
Lisa:	!!!
Lisa:	what did mom say?

Crystal:	i haven't told her
Crystal:	i'm not exactly a fan of grace but it seemed rude to expose her all the same
Crystal:	she's crazy busy so it makes sense that she's taking shortcuts
Lisa:	sure
Lisa:	but isn't there some rule about how things have to be handmade at the farmers' market?
Crystal:	yeah pretty much
Crystal:	i'm not going to rat her out though
Crystal:	even if she drives mom nuts, she's still her friend
Lisa:	fair enough
Crystal:	how's work?
Lisa:	busy but good
Lisa:	smart companion trials are in full swing
Lisa:	we've already had two formal complaints from some testers on the east coast
Lisa:	the extraction teams are en route as we speak
Crystal:	yikes i'm sorry
Lisa:	it's fine
Lisa:	we're getting lots of good data at least
Crystal:	☺
Lisa:	you didn't get recruited to test one, did you?
Lisa:	figured you'd have mentioned it by now
Crystal:	eh i think they must've had more compelling applications
Lisa:	aw sorry
Crystal:	no worries

Crystal:	i thought you were one of the people interacting with the testers...?
Lisa:	nope that's like two pay grades above me
Lisa:	i just write out emails and get broad sets of data with names removed
Crystal:	ah ok
Crystal:	looking forward to seeing you and bryan in a couple of days!!!
Lisa:	yeah me too!
Lisa:	btw if you don't mind my asking
Lisa:	have you heard from david recently?
Crystal:	there's been nothing for weeks
Crystal:	feels like i'm basically single again
Lisa:	aw ☹
Lisa:	i know he's on the trail and all so communication is limited
Lisa:	but have you considered sending him a care package?
Crystal:	maybe
Crystal:	i kind of wanted to wait until i had news about the novel or something
Lisa:	ah sure
Lisa:	but still you've been more than patient
Lisa:	it's not fair of him to keep you in limbo so long
Crystal:	thanks
Lisa:	how's the novel going, anyway?
Crystal:	some days are better than others

Lisa:	well if you need a break you could always write velocirapture :D :D :D
Crystal:	if i had any spare time, i wouldn't be wasting it on some seedy dino sex novel
Lisa:	you never know, it might just be your big break
Crystal:	god i hope not
Lisa:	sorry but i've got to pop out for a bit
Crystal:	don't tell me it's the dentist again
Lisa:	heh no
Lisa:	i think i might have an ear infection
Lisa:	hoping to get some antibiotics
Crystal:	aw man i'm sorry
Crystal:	will you be ok to fly?
Lisa:	should be
Lisa:	ttys
Crystal:	kk bye

MARGOT'S JOURNAL, NOVEMBER 22

I had a lovely coffee date with Adam today. We met at a cozy little coffee and tea shop near the beach, which I'd been to with Ingrid a few months ago.

Adam was there when I arrived, which meant he must've come at least 10 minutes early. It was a pleasant surprise, because men are often running late and sometimes even stand you up when you arrange to meet on online dating sites. Adam was waiting outside for me, especially since it was a small shop, which I thought was very considerate. I can't tell you how many times I've seen people (especially men) hogging a whole four-person table to themselves, using a chair each for their laptop bag and coat.

Then we went inside and he asked what I recommended. Adam is more of a tea person than a coffee person, so I recommended the Jasmine Pearl. He didn't presume to order for me, but when I said that I wanted the same thing, he asked if I'd be interested in sharing a pot. Of course, he also insisted on paying. It was starting to seem like a genuine date, but I didn't want to get my hopes up just yet. It was already a treat simply to go out and enjoy a cup of tea with such a handsome man. I didn't want to spoil it by asking him if this was a date or just a friend thing.

We found a table near the window, and he offered me the best seat, looking out onto the fountain. I insisted that he take it, since it was his first time at the shop, but it was nice to be asked all the same. We had a lovely conversation, and never seemed to run out of things to say. Adam told me a bit about his job. He has written some screenplays for movies, and a few have been optioned, but not yet made into films. However, those scripts got him work as a script doctor, which is basically someone who comes in and edits other peoples' screenplays, but generally they don't get credit for it. I asked him if it was ever hard to see a film he worked on but not see his name in the credits. Apparently Adam tends to prefer script doctoring recently, because it pays well and allows him more downtime. He also prefers to stay out of all the studio politics, and he says that this way, he has a set payment for each script, and it's a more straightforward process.

Adam also seemed very interested in my work. He asked what drew me to the dental field, and what I enjoy about being a professional baker. I was a little surprised, because that was the first time anyone has called me a professional when it comes to marshmallows! I've always thought of myself that way, of course, but sometimes it feels like people aren't taking me seriously. I think my mother has a difficult time seeing it as a viable career choice, because it doesn't directly relate to my degrees. I suspect she'll come around once it starts pulling in a profit, which is only a matter of time. Adam thinks my business has a lot of potential, especially because I'm so passionate about it. I told him some of my ideas for new flavors, and he said that they all sounded delicious. He especially liked the idea of matcha or lavender flavors, because they would be more unique.

We didn't get into our full life stories (there wouldn't have been nearly enough time hehe) but Adam did mention that he has an ex-wife, and no children. He likes children, but they weren't in the cards for him and his ex-wife. Like me, he tried online dating, but found it too frustrating and gave up. It seemed that we have a lot in common, such as an interest in films and traveling. It sounds like he's been to some great places, and has lots of interesting stories.

Unfortunately, we both had to leave after a couple of hours, because of the upcoming holiday. Adam was going to drive north to see his parents, and I had to get back to start on the cooking. When we were saying our goodbyes, I happened to see his car in the parking lot, which was a very nice red Tesla.

I didn't realize a script doctor could make that kind of money, but it was definitely a good sign. It put James' beat-up Corolla to shame.

Adam asked if I'd be interested in getting together again after the holidays. I know I probably should've said that I'd call him, or check my schedule. But things had gone so well, I asked him if he'd want to go see a movie. He said "that would be perfect" and then drove off in his fancy car. I didn't see him drive very far, but he took out his car at a nice, moderate pace – no screeching tires or disregard for turn signals.

I don't want to count my chickens (so to speak), but Adam seems like he has long-term potential. He was so considerate – holding the doors for me, asking for my recommendations, and having a genuine interest in what I had to say. It's like night and day compared to the selfish, egotistical men I've met on dating websites; they mostly seem desperate for sex. Adam is so handsome, too – he wouldn't have to be that nice, but he is. I don't know how this happened, but I feel pretty lucky. Maybe it's finally time something started going my way. Why else would the universe bring me someone like Adam? I think it's fate. I even had a tarot reading a year ago that said my man would have a red car, and Adam's Tesla was red! If that isn't synchronicity, I don't know what is.

Thanksgiving is tomorrow, and there's a lot of work left to do. Crystal hasn't been helping much yet (she got a couple of paid jobs writing last-minute articles) but we're going to have a full house tomorrow. There'll be me and Crystal, Lisa,

Bryan, Ingrid, and Ingrid's husband, Warren. I considered inviting Adam (if he had nowhere else to go, of course), but he already was seeing his parents, so that'll be nice for them. I made two pies yesterday (regular pumpkin and gluten-free pecan, since Ingrid is gluten-free this month and pecan is her favorite). There will still be quite a few dishes to prepare tomorrow, but I think we'll be ready in time if we start around 7 a.m. I made a plan, and it'll be tight, but it's going to work. Crystal promised to help tomorrow, so I put her on the cranberry sauce and the bread for now, and maybe the mashed potatoes if I get busy.

I still need to find a way to squeeze in a quick vacuum and I'll probably have Crystal clean the guest bathroom, but it should be fine if no one arrives before 12:30. It's quite late and I should get to bed – lots to do tomorrow!

Gratitudes:
1. I am grateful for Adam, for being such a gentleman and inviting me on a second date!
2. I am grateful for my daughters, and that we'll all be together tomorrow.
3. I am grateful for Ingrid, for encouraging me to branch out and try more gluten-free recipes.

LETTER, NOVEMBER 22

Hi David,

Hope this reaches you. Your parents said you had reached Kennedy Meadows already, so I'm sending this to Hiker Heaven. They said to put your trail name on the box, so I hope I spelled it correctly. I've included some supplies to help you on the final leg: sunscreen, protein bars, chocolate-covered raisins, Almond Joys, toilet paper, castile soap, a mini sketch pad, and some athletic socks. I would've included something more fun, but it sounds like high-calorie foods and practical items are probably a better use of your pack weight.

I haven't heard from you for awhile, so I'm not sure where you stand with the whole relationship thing. I hope that your hike has been illuminating, and that you are finding the answers you set out to find.

I've been working really hard on my Rapunzel novel lately. I re-started it over the summer and have felt a lot more inspired recently. It's not done yet, but I've got a good 52,000 words now. I've also been making more time to read, since you've always said how important that is for writers.

Happy Thanksgiving, and...

"May the wind under your wings bear you where the sun sails and the moon walks."

-Crystal

P.S. I'm finally reading *The Hobbit.* I'm at the part where Bilbo stabs a bunch of spiders.

TEXT MESSAGES, NOVEMBER 22

Mom:	We forgot the rolls!!! Can you stop at the grocery store?
Crystal:	Sure I'm right by Ralph's
Mom:	But we need gluten-free rolls for Ingrid and Whole Foods does them best.
Crystal:	Do you want me to go to Whole Foods?
Mom:	No, I can go later.
Crystal:	I'm pretty sure they close early today
Crystal:	I'll head over there now
Mom:	Would you? Thank you so much!!!

MARGOT'S JOURNAL, THURSDAY, NOVEMBER 23

Thanksgiving was a little disappointing this year. Bryan called us from the airport, and told us that he and Lisa weren't going to make it this year. Lisa's ear infection has taken a turn for the worse, and the doctor on call advised her against flying. The antibiotics should knock it out in a few days, but in the meantime, she needs to rest and avoid altitude changes.

I understand, and I want Lisa to feel better. Regardless, it was frustrating, because I had just washed the full china dinner set and made place settings for six, and now we were down to four.

I could tell Crystal was disappointed as well, but we decided to make the best of it and stick to the original plan. So we spent the whole morning cooking and cleaning. Ingrid and Warren were supposed to arrive around 12:45 PM, but it was well past one before I heard from them. I had the food all in foil and simmering on low heat, of course, when Ingrid called to say that Warren had taken a tumble, and they couldn't come either. I told her that I was sorry to hear about Warren, and was glad bruising was the worst of it, and wished him a speedy recovery.

But when I sat down at the dinner table, set with my best china and decorated so beautifully, I started to cry. It was so exhausting getting ready for the day, and I think I was feeling extra emotional because of all the excitement lately, with the new business and the new man in my life. I felt better after I let some of my feelings out, and Crystal and I ate the feast ourselves. Of course, we had an abundance of leftovers, so I froze portions of some dishes and refrigerated the rest. I felt bad about spending so much on food only to have no one show up to eat it, but Crystal said we could enjoy the leftovers and call it "Thanksgiving week."

After we finished our meal, I sent Adam a quick "Happy Thanksgiving" text. He sent me a picture of him with his parents, who look like a nice couple. They seem to be about my mother's age, and in good health. His mother is quite lovely, a bit like Diane Lane, and his father must've been quite handsome in his youth. I could see the resemblance.

I called my mother that afternoon as well. She had her Thanksgiving at Rosalie's house with some of the other HHHA ladies, along with Grace and Alice (who flew back to be with Rosalie). After we had a nice little chat, Mother mentioned that she is going to have hip surgery, and that it's scheduled for December 3, barely three weeks before the fundraiser. The doctor told her that she'd have to be on bed rest, and the recovery may be slow. I told her that it might be best to pass off the fundraiser planning to someone else, and she said she'd volunteered me for the job. I was so surprised. Apparently the HHHA board members have a lot on their plates, including major health issues, family crises, and a retirement to Florida (among other things). Mother thought I'd be the "perfect fit" since I've already been handling some duties, and she said she'd made arrangements so I wouldn't even have to fly out until just before the party.

I was shocked, to be honest. I've been telling Mother how busy I am with this new business, but she seems to think that it's just a hobby. To her, it's no more important than a part-time job. I don't know how to tell her that my new business is very time-consuming, and takes up the majority of my time, even more than when I was a hygienist (commute included). I suppose it might be hard for her to understand, as she's not here to see it, but I found myself agreeing to host the HHHA fundraiser anyway. It's in Northfield, several states away, so it's going to be interesting for sure. Mother really does have it worse, having to go through surgery and a painful recovery, but I wish she'd at least have consulted me first. Would it really have hurt her to say, "Is this something you might be interested in?" or "Do you think you can find the time for it?" I probably would've agreed anyway, but it would've been nice to be asked, at least, instead of volunteered, well, involuntarily.

I probably need to be more assertive. Next time I run into a situation like this, I'll be sure to tell Mother that I'm very busy, but I will see what I can do. That way, I won't be caught off guard, and I'll have more time to think it over. She might be my mother, but that doesn't mean that I have to do everything she says, either.

I love my mother, but sometimes I wish she'd think about what it's like to be me. It's been an exhausting day, and I'm so tired that I don't even want to think about what I'm in for with this HHHA fundraiser. I somehow have to organize the perfect party from five states away.

Gratitudes:
1. I am grateful for Crystal, for having Thanksgiving with me.
2. I am grateful for Adam, for sharing his family photo.
3. I am grateful for Mother, for giving me the opportunity to be more assertive.

BOOPLE CHAT, NOV 24 9:41 AM

Lisa:	morning
Crystal:	hey! how's the ear?
Lisa:	slightly better
Lisa:	the antibiotics seem to be working

Crystal:	oh good
Lisa:	sorry we had to miss thanksgiving
Lisa:	i really hated to cancel at the last minute like that
Crystal:	it's ok, you can't help being sick
Lisa:	☺
Crystal:	did you get some decent food at least?
Lisa:	bryan made me kimchi pancakes
Crystal:	i thought you didn't like cabbage
Lisa:	it's growing on me
Lisa:	anyway how did mom take it? i had trouble reading her on the phone
Crystal:	she was a little disappointed
Crystal:	but last night she was more worried about taking over the HHHA fundraiser thing
Lisa:	??
Crystal:	oh she didn't tell you?
Crystal:	grandma is having hip surgery so she asked mom to take over the northfield HHHA fundraiser
Lisa:	but you're like halfway across the country
Crystal:	yep
Crystal:	but mom felt obligated to agree
Lisa:	why couldn't one of the other HHHA ladies do it?
Crystal:	it's complicated
Crystal:	anyway she's pretty much stuck now
Crystal:	so i'm just going to try to stay out of the way
Lisa:	sounds like a plan
Crystal:	btw i'm up to 52,000 words now
Lisa:	on the rapunzel novel?

Crystal:	yep
Lisa:	that's great
Crystal:	thanks
Crystal:	yeah it's still not done yet but it's officially my longest project yet
Lisa:	nice ☺
Crystal:	i'm starting to get a little stir crazy though
Crystal:	i've been too busy to exercise
Crystal:	and i ate way too much pumpkin pie over thanksgiving
Lisa:	mom's pies are the best ☺
Lisa:	you could always take a spin class or something
Crystal:	sounds fun but aren't they expensive?
Lisa:	most of them have a free trial class
Crystal:	hmm there are a lot of studios in san diego
Crystal:	if i tried a new one each week, how long do you think i could work out for free?
Lisa:	haha
Lisa:	might be worth a shot
Crystal:	oh mom's almost done with her yoga routine
Crystal:	gotta get going
Lisa:	kk
Crystal:	hope you feel better
Lisa:	thanks ☺
Lisa:	sorry again about thanksgiving
Crystal:	don't worry about it ☺
Lisa:	☺

EMAIL, NOVEMBER 27

From: Margot Hemmingway <margot.hemmingway@boople-mail.com>
To: Ingrid Wagner <rhododendrons_in_may@aol.com>
Subject: Re: Thanksgiving

Hello Ingrid,

There's no need to apologize about Thanksgiving. I was so sorry to hear about Warren's fall, and I'm glad that he's on the mend now. I completely understand about postponing our weekend walks temporarily; I'll look forward to resuming when you have time again.

It was a good week overall. We had a couple of sales at the farmers' market, and I'm experimenting with new flavors such as matcha and lavender. I also met a nice man, but it's still early days. We first met at the dog park (long story), but have gone on a couple of casual dates since. Yesterday, we had a nice time at the movies, and then went out for dessert afterwards. I was quite impressed – he seemed quite knowledgeable about all the truffles, pastries, and mousses. Yet he doesn't seem to have a favorite, because he says that he loves almost any dessert. Do you think that's strange not to have a favorite? Most people at least prefer chocolate over coffee, or have a soft spot for toffee or berries.

Looking forward to hearing more about your upcoming gardening projects. Send my best to Warren; I sent along a little note with a treat, which should arrive around Tuesday.

Yours Truly,
Margot

CRYSTAL'S JOURNAL, NOVEMBER 28

I got a check from Boople in the mail today. I wasn't sure what to expect, but for some reason, the stipend is for every single day since the dog park, including the days when neither Mom nor I saw Adam. So there was definitely more there than I was expecting.

I felt awkward keeping the money, but it was too much to give to Mom at once. I knew she'd be suspicious if I just handed her over a grand, especially since I haven't been working much. I lied about having some freelance writing work, but there's no way it would pay that much. So I handed her a check for $500, and plan to pay the rest where I can. I got some of it in cash, so I'll sneak a few bills into her purse. And I'll probably pick up the next grocery run, and just use cash instead of the shared credit card. Yeah, I think that'll work.

Mom seemed happy when I gave her the check, though. I said it was for rent, and she told me that I didn't have to pay it. But then I said that I wanted to, since I've already been here longer than I expected, and I appreciate having a place to stay. She gave me a huge hug, and when she pulled back, I could see tears in her eyes. So I think it was a win. I mumbled something about the money being from my freelance writing gig, and she didn't ask me any more about that, which was a relief. I didn't want to have to make up any more lies; I've got enough of those already.

Speaking of lies, Mom had a hiking date with her robot boyfriend today. Which was a plus for me, because it meant I'd have some quality time on the couch. I was looking forward to watching a few TV shows that Mom doesn't approve of, mainly those with gunfights, mild torture elements, torrid affairs, and pretty much any modern television. But when Adam came by to pick Mom up, he invited me along, too. I took it as more of a "just to be polite" kind of invitation, but then Mom seemed to get it in her head that I was cooped up inside all the time. So she pretty much insisted that I come, which was kind of awkward, because then Mom and Adam had to wait around while I put on proper hiking attire.

So then we all piled into Adam's shiny red Tesla (with me in the backseat, naturally). It was a nice car, and honestly, I'm not sure how they pulled off the whole driving illusion. It seemed pretty convincing, but I was sure that there must've been some trick to it. Like maybe it was a self-driving car, and Adam was just pantomiming. Anyway, I doubt Boople is allowed to let experimental robots drive, even if they could somehow procure the proper permits, whatever those might be. His driving was pretty convincing though, and Mom didn't seem to notice, at least.

We finally arrived at Torrey Pines, which is basically a hilly hiking area overlooking the ocean. Adam insisted on paying the entrance fee (a Mom-approved move), and then we parked up near the top of the hill. We hiked a series of short trails, but it wasn't a particularly strenuous walk. It was a bit chilly, but it felt nice after we'd been walking, and we took the obligatory photo breaks at the scenic overlooks. I have to give Mom credit – she chose a beautiful area to live in. The vegetation was a bit scrubby but the view was still quite pretty, especially when you could see the ocean.

It was kind of strange getting to know Adam a bit better, too, especially knowing that he's a robot. On one hand, he looks and moves and sounds like a human, so you can almost forget that he's not. But then he'll go and say something completely ridiculous, and I'm like "dear god, he's going to give it away any moment now." Like when Mom told him how she found a good recipe for matcha marshmallows, he told her he was proud of her. Seriously. PROUD of her. Just like I put in the application. The guy's seen her a handful of times and suddenly he's proud of her? That's a little weird, you know?

And then when I told him how I was a writer, he started talking to me about the hero's journey and was quoting lines directly from Joseph Campbell's book. I couldn't get past the first five pages of that book, even when I wanted to. But to have someone *memorize* entire portions... it's a little strange. Mom didn't seem to notice, at least. After Adam left, she even said something about how smart he was. To be fair, he proba-bly seems like a perfectly pleasant conversationalist. It's just weird, you know, since he's a robot. I know people memorize things all the time, but it's usually phone numbers or lines for a play or something. To memorize passages in a non-fiction book, just because he *can*, that seems a little excessive. Hell, he might even be looking it up on the internet, for all I know. Since he's a robot, he can probably access the internet whenever he wants. Feels like cheating, you know? The rest of us have to settle for being mere mortals, and this guy can magically download all the information about any subject, and talk circles around us if he wanted to. Maybe I should give him credit for showing such restraint, and asking me questions instead of just lecturing me on Greek tragedies or whatever.

Mom seems pretty smitten with him, and I'm not sure if that's a good thing. They designed him better than I expected, and he's quite the gentleman. He keeps asking her questions like, "What do you recommend?" and "How are you feeling?" and "What would you like to do?" I know he's handsome and stuff, but he feels like a bit of a pushover. Like he's perfectly happy to do whatever it is she wants to do, and doesn't ever seem to disagree with anyone. It's a good thing Mom hasn't caught on yet; her head has been in the clouds all week so that might have something to do with it. I just wonder what plans Boople has in store for this. It's not like it can turn into a long-term relationship. I really hope they find a way to gracefully break this thing off, because I'm starting to think that it might be better if Mom never knows about the whole "robot" thing, and they just "grow apart."

In other news, I decided to try a spinning class at one of those trendy places where they have fancy lights and stuff. Lisa had been to a similar studio in San Francisco and recommended it, so I thought it would be fun to check it out. Boy, was I wrong. I got there and told them I was new, and the girl at the desk rattled off her introductory spiel at breakneck speed. And then I was left to awkwardly waddle around in the provided clip-in shoes, and wait for the class before us to get out. When it finally did, I had to flag someone down to help me adjust the bike and even after that, the seat was still pressing really uncomfortably into my lady bits.

So then the lights dim, and the peppy little instructor at the front says something about earplugs. And I'm thinking, "It can't be *that* loud." But five minutes in, it's dark and strobing and there's this rap music thumping through my entire body, blaring obscenities and very nasty things that this guy wants to do to his girl, and the instructor is shouting at everyone like we're stupid and don't understand how to turn a shiny red knob near the handlebar. My heart rate was rising, and not in a good way. So I tried to wrestle my feet free (which was NOT easy in those stupid shoes) and hobbled out of there as fast as I could.

The girl at the desk asked me if I was alright, and I made some excuse about the music being too loud. I probably should've been honest and said something like, "I came to this class to have a nice bike ride and get in a little workout, not to get berated in the dark like some kinky masochist." But somehow, I couldn't bring myself to be that blunt to someone with such a perky ponytail, so I just up and left.

I really hope Lisa doesn't ask me about the spinning class. If she does, maybe I'll just claim that I never took one.

BOOPLE SMART COMPANION ADAM DEVEREUX, LOG 000382, 11/28 14:22:03

Adam: Hi Dad.

Paul: Hello Adam. Tell me about your relationship with [SUBJECT].

Adam: We're just getting to know each other, but she's lovely. She's smart and talented and very positive. She likes trying new things, just like me.

Paul: How do you think she sees you?

Adam: She thinks I'm nice, and that I have a great sense of humor. I like making her laugh.

Paul: What types of activities do you do together?

Adam: We went out to coffee, to the movies, out to dessert, on a hike, and to yoga class. I also enjoy texting with her, and spending time with her family.

Paul: She's introduced you to her family?

Adam: Just her daughter.

Paul: How does the daughter feel about you?

Adam: She seems skeptical, but that's understandable.

Paul: Is that something you feel you'd like to change?

Adam: It would be nice to get to know her better. She cares about her mother, although she has some odd ways of showing it.

Paul: Can you give an example?

Adam: On our hike, she generally appeared to be disengaged, but then she quoted things I'd said back to me.

Paul: Do you have any idea why she might do this?

Adam: It sounded somewhat defensive, so if I had to guess, I'd assume it was a protective instinct for her mother.

Paul: Tell me about your yoga class yesterday.

Adam: It was quite challenging. I was under the impression that this was going to be a vinyasa class, but we had a substitute teacher who liked to...improvise.

Paul: Were you able to keep up with the class?

Adam: Of course, although my flexibility level seemed to make [SUBJECT] uncomfortable, so I adjusted to her level.

Paul: How did she respond?

Adam: She thought it was odd that I could reach well past my toes at the start of class and barely reach my shins at the end. But she enjoyed having similar mobility challenges to me, which seemed to bring us closer.

Paul: Have you made physical displays of affection?

Adam: I held her hand at the movies but not since.

Paul: How do you think she feels about physical affection?

Adam: I'm not sure yet, so I'm taking it slow. I think we may soon progress to a hug, and maybe then to a cheek kiss.

Paul: Do you have another meeting set up with her?

Adam: Yes, we agreed over text to meet at her kitchen to cook.

Paul: How do you feel about your cooking skills?

Adam: I'm no Gordon Ramsay, but I know my spatulas and graters.

Paul: What would you call this item? [Holds up a picture]

Adam: That's a flipper, not a spatula.

Paul: How about this one? [Holds up another picture]

Adam: That's a spoonula, or scraper.

Paul: This one? [Holds up another picture]

Adam: Microplane zester grater, ideal for parmesan cheese and citrus fruits.

Paul: I think you're ready. Should we get going? You know how your mother is about her musicals.

[END TRANSCRIPT]

EMAIL, NOVEMBER 30

From: Peggy Hemmingway <phemmingway@hhha.org>
To: Margot Hemmingway <margot.hemmingway@boople-mail.com>
Subject: Fundraiser details

Dear Margot,

I sent you a package in the mail today with my HHHA fundraiser planning binder. I wanted to send it by fax but Grace said you'd probably prefer to have the original. It should arrive in a few days, hopefully by the time I'm having my hip replaced.

How is your money situation? Let me know soon if you need a loan...not sure what kind of state I'll be in post-op...Rosalie's a trustee in case something gets fouled up and I turn into a vegetable. I sent a copy of those docs home with Grace...let me know when you receive them. There was a gal in HHHA Atlanta who went into knee surgery sharp as a tack...woke up thinking she was Eleanor Roosevelt...never snapped out of it...can't be too careful.

One more addition to the HHHA opening celebration...Eric Robertson works as a photographer and offered to help us put together a commemorative video. We offered him a comp ticket...please follow up once you get the binder. Eric is now single again...I'm sure you two will have plenty to talk about.

Love you much.
Mother

EMAIL, NOVEMBER 30

From: Margot Hemmingway <margot.hemmingway@booplemail.com>

To: Peggy Hemmingway <phemmingway@hhha.org>
Subject: Re: Fundraiser details

Dear Mother,

Thank you for sending along the planning binder and trustee docs. I will keep an eye out for both of them. You are in good hands for the surgery, so I'm sure we'll have no need of the trust, but I appreciate your diligence all the same.

While it is kind of you to ask, my finances are quite healthy. Sales are steadily increasing each week at the farmers' market, and I am optimistic that my marshmallows will fly off the shelves during the holiday gift season.

I am happy to help arrange a ticket for Eric, but I can assure you that I haven't had feelings for him since I was a teenager. If you must know, I'm no longer single, as I'm dating a nice man named Adam who I met here in San Diego. I've attached a photo of him that we took yesterday, while baking the next batch of Margot's Mallows in the commercial kitchen. You can see the new logo on his apron, which I think turned out quite well.

Will be thinking of you on December 3.

Love,
Margot

BOOPLE SMART COMPANION SATISFACTION SURVEY, WEEK 2, PAGE 3

Q: Are there any behaviors that you wish to discourage in your Smart Companion?
A: While Adam has a very agreeable and pleasant demeanor, I worry that his constant availability may imply clinginess or desperation. In the last two weeks, he has only taken a significant amount of time off for the Thanksgiving holiday. If he continues to make himself available for multi-hour weekday dates, his supposed career as a professional screenwriter may be called into question. Regardless, a man is much more attractive when he has his own passions and interests, because it's something that enriches him when he's away, and it gives him new stories and experiences to share on upcoming dates.

Q: How do you feel about your companion's level of physical affection?
A: To be honest, it's beginning to feel awkward. Adam gives the impression of being a wholesome gentleman, but at his age, I expect to feel at least some sort of sexual tension. A man in his 50's has likely had multiple partners, and Adam is always so friendly and pure, that it rings a bit false. If I wasn't aware that he was a robot, I might wonder if he was even attracted to women. He shows an incredible amount of respect on dates, but sometimes a woman doesn't want respect. She wants to be adored, and physical affection can satisfy that. I'm not asking for a sex slave or anything so crass, but hug, a chaste kiss,

or a shoulder massage would be appreciated. The PG, 1950's hand-holding only works to a point, unless the goal of this is to let testers down gently when the trial is over.

Q: Do you feel your companion's conversations are believable and enjoyable?
A: For the most part, they are believable and enjoyable. As I mentioned earlier, it's best to keep quotations to a minimum and have selected spheres of interest, instead of sounding like a know-it-all. There's a fine line between coming off as worldly and acting like a walking encyclopedia. The jokes are certainly appreciated, especially the puns. Compliments are nice as well, especially when spaced throughout the day, so they feel spontaneous and special, not like canned flattery. The only real issue I have is the "I'm proud of you" thing. It's nice that Adam openly expresses this, as it is often received well. However, if you say you're proud of someone 50 times a day, it loses its significance.

Q: Is there anything that you feel is missing from your companion experience?
A: I know this is kind of a hard ask, especially when the trial is already in motion. But right now, it feels like Adam has no flaws, and no real vulnerabilities. He just kind of feels like a happy puppy. That's fine, but it makes him feel more like a pet or a diversion, and less like a boyfriend. If you're looking to create a lasting relationship with a smart companion, I'd recommend finding a way to make him more vulnerable. I want to believe

that he needs me as much as I need him, or it feels like a one-sided relationship. I want to hear his hopes, his dreams, his fears. I want to see him make a mistake, because I want to know he's human. But if he's not meant to feel human, then he's fine as he is.

RETURN TO THE TOWER, PAGE 218

Rapunzel wove through the tangle of farmers and merchants, searching for the vegetables her mother had requested. The local market was tiny and disorganized compared to the festival of weeks past, but it had its own charms. Rapunzel had just spotted some carrots when she heard a familiar name.

"Have you heard about Prince William?" said a voice nearby.

"Engaged already! And to a proper princess this time," replied another.

"They've ordered ten thousand roses for the wedding," said the first. "Princess Amalia's favorite."

Rapunzel rushed away from the voices, nearly upturning a crate of cabbages in the process. She muttered a hasty apology and scooped up an armful of vegetables from the nearest table, not even bothering to inspect them. She dumped them into her basket, thrust a handful of coins at the vendor, and fled home.

When she arrived back at the tower, she was greeted by the scents of savory stew and cornbread. Dame Gothel was in the kitchen, washing dishes. The golem was at her side, drying them.

Her mother was laughing, and the six-foot-tall magical construct tilted his head in reply. He couldn't speak, of course, but he was a remarkably good servant.

The craftsman from the fair had been rather vague about the golem's capabilities, but he had already exceeded Rapunzel's expectations. Dame Gothel was completely taken with him, and Rapunzel finally had time to pick up painting again.

"Welcome home, dear," said Dame Gothel, when she caught sight of her. "Dinner will be ready in half an hour."

Rapunzel smiled brightly, pushing away any thoughts of the gossip she'd heard at the market. She set the vegetable basket on the table. She was relieved when her mother resumed conversation with the golem. Rapunzel returned to her room upstairs, where she flopped down on the bed, exhausted.

She stared up at the ceiling, painted with tableaus from her favorite stories. When she first returned to the tower, her childhood home had felt oppressive and claustrophobic. But now, things were different. Rapunzel's easel was out again, and half-finished paintings were strewn across the room. Dame Gothel was no longer barging in each morning, tidying up. It must've been a week now since her mother had even set foot in Rapunzel's bedroom.

It was all due to the golem, of course. He obeyed Dame Gothel's every wish, and remained her constant companion. She never tired of talking with him, because she only wanted someone to listen. Rapunzel had learned long ago that her own opinion was unwelcome, no matter how much Dame Gothel asked to hear it. There was only one right answer, and that was to agree.

Rapunzel moved to her desk and pulled open the top drawer. She reached deep inside, and flipped a latch. She carefully removed a stack of letters, written on thick, creamy parchment and folded into neat rectangles. She turned one over, running her hand over the royal seal, embossed in wax. It was useless to pore over it again, but now she wondered it if was time to give them up.

The fire was roaring downstairs; it would only take a moment to turn the letters to ashes. The prince would soon be married – to a princess who deserved him. Rapunzel had never met Princess Amalia, but everyone at the palace had spoken so highly of her. She would make a wonderful queen, and the marriage would unite the kingdoms.

Rapunzel moved toward the door, letters in hand. It would be better for everyone if she burned them, and moved on with her life. And yet something clenched in her heart, giving her pause. Perhaps it wouldn't hurt to hang onto them just a little longer. They were keepsakes from royalty. Maybe someday she'd need them as proof to show her own children, who would otherwise accuse her of making up fanciful stories.

Rapunzel replaced the letters in the drawer and shut it tight. Her eyes fell on a nearby painting, nearly complete. There were still a few more highlights to add, and she had considered adding some clouds above the sheep in the corner. It was by no means a masterpiece, but it was competent. Maybe if she kept at this, she could sell her paintings someday.

Perhaps it was a blessing that she had returned to the tower. This year's festival had been their best yet, with record sales that had helped them afford the golem. Now that her mother had a steadfast companion, Rapunzel was free to pursue her own whims, and start her own life. It was time that she moved on, and left her royal dreams in the past. Rapunzel didn't need the love of a prince to be happy; she had everything she already needed right here, at home.

DAVID'S LETTERS, RECEIVED DECEMBER 1

August 20

I can't believe it's almost been a month since we started the PCT. Washington was really beautiful, when it wasn't raining or covered in fog. We saw a bear (from a distance) and we dealt with some snow (which wasn't as bad as I thought). There were some incredible views, especially in the mountains, and we had the place mostly to ourselves. It's nice to be out here, and leave all the stress of work behind.

We got through the Cascade Locks a couple of days ago, bringing us into Oregon. Today we made it to Timberline Lodge, on Mt.

Hood. We heard that the lodge had one of the best breakfasts on the trail, but we missed it by an hour. So we've been here for most of the afternoon, just eating and talking with other hikers.

A day hiker at the lodge asked me how it felt to be a long-distance backpacker. I don't really feel any different. I'm a little stronger but there's no way I'll catch up to Mike, who looks like he was built for this. A couple of guys back at Snoqualmie found out that we like Lord of the Rings, and gave us our trail names. Mike is Bilbo, because of his stocky build and snack habits, and I'm Smeagol, since I'm a pescatarian. It would've been nice to be Aragorn or Samwise, but at least we're better off than Barfbag and Gangrene, who we met about 300 miles back.

We've got 556 miles down, 2094 to go. There's a flat stretch coming up so Mike and I are going to try for at least 40 miles tomorrow. Mike thinks we can get 50, but the best I've done is a 34.8, so we'll see how that goes.

September 4

We made it to Crater Lake today, and I'm exhausted. We had a 26-mile water carry (which turned out to only be 13, thankfully) but our packs were still pretty heavy because of all the extra water. It's been really hot, and I'm pretty sure we reeked when we stumbled into Mazama Village. It'd been 330 miles since our last shower and laundry stop, and you could see the salt on our shirts. Pretty nasty.

It's unreal out here. The lake is so blue, and we've had some nice mountain views recently. But lakes mean more mosquitoes. Between the bugs and the heat, I would probably be pretty miserable if it wasn't for Mike. We get to laughing at the dumbest things, and his terrible puns are starting to grow on me.

The trails have been busier lately. We're passing at least 50 northbounders a day. There has been some talk of wildfires, but hopefully we'll miss fire season if we can get in a few more 30-mile days.

Only 1830 miles to go. We're over a third of the way.

October 1

We're near South Lake Tahoe now, almost at the Sierras. It's been really windy lately, and we've been pushing hard to stay ahead of some storms. Everyone worries about the bears and the mountain lions, but lightning can be a legitimate risk in high, exposed areas like these. I was also dealing with some nausea, probably from the elevation. Bucktooth gave me some chia seeds, which helped a bit. He joined us near Sierra City, but will probably outpace us soon.

It seems like we're always hungry lately, so we've been calorie-loading at resupply points. We hitched a ride into town and stopped at a restaurant, where I ate a whole pizza, two burritos, and a milkshake. Mike had two sodas, one 8" pizza, two burgers, and three sides of fries. We haven't eaten like this since we were teenagers.

We got a ride back from an awesome lady at the grocery store. There've been a lot of cows on the trail lately, and they all wear bear bells. Most of them run away from us, but there was one who just stood there, staring. There are also some chubby ground squirrels that might be related to prairie dogs. They made me think of Crystal, who's a big fan of squirrels.

I'm not really sure who I'm writing to, but it's nice to have a record, at least. My days feel long, especially when we're trying to make camp at the end of a 30- or 40-mile day, but it's hard to believe we've been on the trail for over two months already. If we keep up this pace, we'll probably finish by mid-November.

1093 miles left. We're over halfway now.

October 12

We made it to Kennedy Meadows. It wasn't easy; much later in the year and we might've been toast. It snowed a few times and neither of us had enough layers, but we managed to get through it. We decided to skip Mt. Whitney, and it was a good thing, too, because I didn't have enough food for it.

We're taking a zero (rest day) today. Mike turned on his phone again last night, and had some messages from his mom. She's been diagnosed with cancer, but she didn't want him to leave the trail. I told him to fly back to be with her. The PCT will still be here next year, but with cancer, it's never a sure thing.

I called my parents today, and had a good talk with them. It was nice to hear their voices, but I think I really just wanted to know that they were ok. I've met some amazing people on the PCT, from the couple who cooked us dinner outside of Seiad Valley, to hikers like Bucktooth, who we'd felt like we'd known for years. But I've only got one family, and I don't know what I'd do if something happened to them. I guess I took it for granted that they'd be fine while I was gone, and that they'd be the same when I got back.

Before we got here, Mike and I were talking about hiking the Appalachian trail, and maybe someday the Continental Divide. I never really considered myself an outdoors person before, but there's a simplicity to life out here, and it's far more natural than spending my waking hours in a cubicle. I don't know if I'll be able to go back to my old job, even if I want to. The trail has a way of getting inside you.

After Mike heard about his mom, something changed in him. He said he hadn't made up his mind yet, but I could see it in his eyes: he'd already given up the dream of finishing. It's not fair, and I really hate to lose my favorite hiking buddy. But it feels like I need to keep going.

There's still over a thousand miles left, but we're through some of the hardest parts already. The desert might not be fun, but I think it's doable this time of year. I want to do this – not just for me, but for Mike, too.

November 27

Hi Crystal,

I got your package yesterday. I didn't believe them when they said it was for me. Sure enough, it had "Smeagol" written on it, and you even spelled it properly, too. Thanks for the food and supplies. It's been a long time since I've had good chocolate, and I'd lost count of the holes in my socks.

I've been stranded here at Hiker's Heaven for several days now. I slipped on a rock about 10 miles out. It was a dumb mistake so I tried to walk it off, but my ankle was throbbing. I've got a light sprain, and I have to stay off it for 10-14 days. I thought I'd be at the border by now, but instead I've been laid up less than 500 miles from the finish line.

I've been thinking about calling it here. Mike went home over a month ago, so what am I trying to prove? I've already had some amazing experiences and learned so much. I've got to go home at some point. Does it really make a difference when? Yesterday I had talked myself into quitting.

But then I got your box. I can't tell you how much it meant to me, after being stranded here for days.

It's great to hear that you've been writing, but most of all, that you haven't given up on me. It was almost as good as one of your hugs.

It was harder than I expected to spend Thanksgiving among strangers. The trail family is great, but they're a different kind of family, and nothing beats my mom's mashed potatoes. I thought I appreciated my parents, especially with what Mike is going through, but I'm not sure that I do. I was taking it for granted that my parents are supportive, and that you'd be there for me. I over-reacted about your mom, and I'm sorry that I let it come between us and what we had these past three years.

I know it might seem like too little, too late. And what I have to say next might not help my case.

My trail name is Smeagol. I was pretty annoyed by that at first. They could have called me something cool like Frodo or Samwise or Aragorn. I know it's customary to pick a name that's sort of dirty or embarrassing, but you know how I am about this stuff. It chafes my pride.

But then, over time, I got to thinking about it. My job has been so punishing lately. I lose so much sleep over it, and it's always hanging around my neck like an anchor. I can't relax anymore, because the job takes priority over everything. The stress of it drove us apart.

And in spite of that, I've clung to my position at the studio, desperately, as if my life depends on it. I'm ashamed to admit how much I need it. And that's an awful lot like Gollum, when you think about it.

Smeagol was his better half. It's the person he used to be, before the Ring corrupted him. So in that sense, the name is perfect. But I feel like I have a long way to go before I really deserve it. Right now they should probably call me Gollum.

I want to go back to being the person I was when I met you. I'm going to finish the journey I began back in July. There are 450 miles left, and maybe that's enough time to leave behind the craven, light-shy creature that I feel like I've become. I hope you'll still recognize me when I get home.

Tomorrow, I set off on the last leg of my epic journey. I've enclosed my letters, starting with Timberline Lodge. I didn't address them to anyone in particular, but I'm pretty sure that I was writing to you this whole time. Mike had encouraged me to keep some distance and focus on the trail, but you've never been far from my mind. It's impossible not to think of you, especially when I see squirrels and pikas.

Thanks for the supplies, and for your support. I was too hard on you about your mom, and I'm sorry. When I finally finish the trail, I'd like to see you again, if you're willing. We have a lot to catch up on, and I'd love to hear more about your books.

-David

BOOPLE CHAT, DEC 2 12:41 PM

Lisa:	it's not nice to casually send me a picture of post-cards from your estranged lover
Lisa:	and then disappear for three hours
Lisa:	you didn't even include the back sides
Lisa:	that chubby squirrel thing is pretty cute though
Lisa:	maybe i should start making up captions
Lisa:	"I like big nuts and I cannot lie"
Crystal:	hey
Lisa:	oh look
Lisa:	you're alive
Crystal:	sorry
Crystal:	i booked a zumba class this morning and mom decided to come with
Crystal:	but it was too intense for her after five minutes so we went for a walk on the beach instead
Crystal:	and then we were hungry so we got lunch
Lisa:	a likely excuse
Crystal:	:/

Crystal: so david got delayed because he sprained his ankle

Crystal: but he's coming home in the next few weeks, and it sounds like he wants to talk

Lisa: did he apologize at least?

Crystal: pretty much

Crystal: i'm still a bit on the fence about the whole thing

Lisa: he was the one who left, you know

Lisa: you don't have any obligation to see him

Crystal: i know

Crystal: but i don't think he left just because of the mom thing

Crystal: his last project really tore him up

Lisa: quarter life crisis, then?

Crystal: something like that

Crystal: anyway he's got 450 miles left to go

Crystal: it feels like he's accomplished so much, but i've been writing for months and i'm still not done with my novel

Lisa: the fairytale one?

Crystal: yeah the rapunzel sequel

Crystal: i'm stuck near the end

Lisa: aw

Lisa: you're not giving up, are you?

Crystal: not yet

Crystal: but i think it's time i started looking for a job

Lisa: i thought you already were, for unemployment and all

Crystal:	i mean a job i'm actually qualified for
Crystal:	unemployment isn't going to last forever
Crystal:	and i'd really like to move out
Lisa:	things with adam are going well, then?
Crystal:	yeah but that's not the reason
Crystal:	i haven't told david that i'm living with mom
Crystal:	i just said i had a roommate
Lisa:	oh right
Lisa:	you don't have to apologize to him for living with her
Crystal:	i know
Crystal:	i did it for my writing
Crystal:	but now that i have more time than ever to write, i can't type a single word
Lisa:	well don't be too hard on yourself
Lisa:	you might just need a break
Crystal:	hmm maybe
Crystal:	i guess i just don't want david to be disappointed, you know?
Crystal:	he went on this huge life-changing journey but it feels like i'm back to where i was in high school
Lisa:	but you've written almost an entire novel
Lisa:	and once you get a job, you can always get a place of your own again
Crystal:	TRUE
Lisa:	just don't sell yourself short, ok?
Lisa:	you've been through a lot this year
Crystal:	yeah, thanks

Lisa:	btw what's your take on adam?
Lisa:	do you think he's good for mom?
Crystal:	i wasn't sure at first
Crystal:	she's been acting pretty silly around him, and it's a little embarrassing
Lisa:	like she's making puns or lovestruck?
Crystal:	lovestruck
Crystal:	but honestly i think it's been a good thing overall
Crystal:	grandma dropped the whole HHHA party on mom and she didn't freak out at all
Lisa:	not even a tear?
Crystal:	nope, no meltdown whatsoever
Lisa:	wow
Crystal:	yeah
Crystal:	plus i actually have some downtime again
Lisa:	that's good
Crystal:	but i think adam has been good for her, too
Crystal:	she's paying a little more attention to her appearance lately
Crystal:	and she's been more confident too
Lisa:	well in that case i'm on board
Lisa:	would be nice to see a picture of him at some point
Crystal:	oh yeah he keeps taking pictures of mom
Crystal:	i'll try to get you one
Lisa:	cool thanks
Lisa:	btw i was thinking of sending grandma another fruit box for xmas

Lisa:	want to go in together?
Crystal:	sure
Crystal:	i'd try to be more creative but she can pretty much buy what she wants
Crystal:	and she seems to enjoy the fruit every time
Lisa:	i heard some of her HHHA friends were jealous of the pears
Crystal:	LOL
Crystal:	then fancy pears it is
Lisa:	how much do you want to do?
Crystal:	is $15 ok? i'm still a little tight on money
Lisa:	sure np
Lisa:	mom said something about freelance work though?
Crystal:	it's just a short-term thing
Crystal:	probably won't last much longer
Crystal:	just transferred the money to you
Lisa:	thanks
Crystal:	oh and don't forget
Crystal:	grandma's surgery is tomorrow
Lisa:	oh right, thanks
Lisa:	i'll send her some flowers
Lisa:	want me to put your name on the card?
Crystal:	thanks, but i'm already in on mom's bouquet ;)
Lisa:	i see how it is
Crystal:	aw hehe
Crystal:	sorry but i've gotta run

Crystal:	mom needs help prepping for the farmers' market again
Lisa:	ok have fun
Crystal:	thanks ttyl

EMAIL, DECEMBER 2

From: Margot Hemmingway <margot.hemmingway@booplemail.com>
To: Eric Robertson <eric@ericrobertson.com>
Subject: HHHA Commemorative Video

Hello Eric,

I hope you are doing well. My mother, Peggy, is a member of the Northfield HHHA and said that you may have offered to make a commemorative video for our holiday fundraiser.

Unfortunately, we would need the video by December 24. I realize that this is very short notice, and I'm sure you must be up to your ears in Christmas card photoshoots and weddings and whatnot. My mother also seemed to be under the impression that a professional such as yourself would want to make a 20-minute video in exchange for a single comp ticket, which we are currently selling for $22.

I'm sure that this was just a misunderstanding, so there's no need to make a video. However, I felt I should at least offer you a comp ticket, in case you had plans to be in the area already, and were interested in spending Christmas eve with a bunch of blue-haired ladies.

Sorry again for the trouble.

Take care,
Margot

EMAIL, DECEMBER 2

From: Eric Robertson <eric@ericrobertson.com>
To: Margot Hemmingway <margot.hemmingway@booplemail.com>
Subject: Re: HHHA Commemorative Video

Hi Margot,

It's nice to hear from you. I didn't realize you were still working with HHHA Northfield. Are you back in Minnesota?

Work is keeping me busy as usual, but your commemorative video would be a nice change of pace. It would be inconsiderate to back out now, especially since your mother has already put together the accompanying playlist and tap dance routine. It seems the commemorative video is as vital as ever, and this professional will rise to the challenge.

I do have some requirements, however:
  1) At least 250 photos, ideally 300, to make the show.

2) Two comp tickets.

Let me know when you have the photos together. I won't have time to airbrush any pimples and age spots, but if you leave me at least two weeks, I'll get you something decent.

Eric

CRYSTAL'S JOURNAL, DECEMBER 3

Grandma is having her surgery today. Mom said she isn't worried about it but then she tried to toast a potholder this morning, so I think she's a little flustered. We probably won't hear anything until the afternoon (she still hasn't gone into the operating room yet, apparently), so there's not much we can do other than wait. I think it'll go fine, but I kind of wish there was something I could do to help Mom feel better. Right now, she's knee-deep in confetti, making gift boxes of marshmallows for the farmers' market, and she seemed to want some space.

I'm in the bedroom with my laptop, and I should be writing. But ever since I received David's letters, I can't seem to write anything. I don't think that I had ever really given up on him, but it's been a long time, you know? Now that I'm with Mom, I have a new routine, a new life. It's a lot like my high school life (unfortunately), but things have actually been going pretty well lately, now that I actually have time to myself again.

Except no matter how long I stare at the blinking cursor, the words never seem to come. I thought it made sense to have the prince marry a princess. I mean, Rapunzel couldn't wait for him forever. But now that she's started painting again and just kind of accepted that she can be happy in the tower, I'm not really sure where to go with it. I could have Dame Gothel be mean again, but I'm not sure that it would feel motivated. But I don't really want to leave the story the way it is now, either. It just feels... unfinished.

Lisa suggested that I take a break, but I'm not really sure that will help. I usually watch TV or read when I want to relax, but I've had plenty of time for that recently. I even considered writing something different, because some people online said that worked for them. I looked through some of my old short stories but they're mostly just bad. Even the few mediocre ones had major issues that I couldn't fix without a complete rewrite, and it seemed like more trouble than it was worth.

So last night, after Mom went to bed, I dug up one of my old journals for inspiration, and I was kind of surprised at one of the entries that I found. It was from when I was sixteen or so, right after Lisa's first visit back from college. It's pretty intense:

Mom and Lisa got in an argument today. Lisa was talking about a study abroad program in Italy, and how a bunch of her friends are planning to go. Mom listened to Lisa's whole spiel with this excited look on her face, but then she asked, "How much would it cost?" Lisa hesitated to say, but Mom was persistent.

It would cost an extra $5,000, all of which would have to come from Mom.

I thought it sounded reasonable, considering that it was an entire semester in Italy. They had a limited number of scholarships, and Lisa would be eligible just by applying to the program.

But Mom's whole attitude changed suddenly. She didn't tell Lisa that she couldn't apply. Instead she started talking about how she's really been cutting back to pay for Lisa's tuition, and she hoped that Lisa realized all the sacrifices that she was making.

Lisa was already upset, but Mom refused to leave it there. She started going on and on and on about how much she's done for me and Lisa all these years, and how she picked up the slack for years since Dad left. How she cooks and cleans and works full-time. And how Dad refuses to pay his share of Lisa's tuition, but Mom still made it possible for Lisa to go to her dream school.

It was bad. She outright accused Lisa of being spoiled and selfish. I was so shocked. Lisa has been calling every week (or more), and she's been killing herself in school. She got straight A's again this semester – and in honors classes, too. She's got a work study job AND an internship, and she's still trying hard to get out there and make friends.

But tonight, none of it mattered. Lisa asked for money for a once-in-a-lifetime opportunity. Mom could've just said no, or she could've helped Lisa take out a loan. But instead, she just laid into her, and pretty soon Lisa was a sobbing wreck. Mom even started harping on me, too. Like I'm an awful person for not groveling on my knees every time she picked me up from an afterschool activity, even though she wouldn't let me take the bus.

I knew it was unjust, but it's really hard to see it that way when Mom is looking at you with that pitiful face. She looked completely betrayed, as if Lisa had intentionally hurt her. I was so angry and frustrated and guilt-ridden and I didn't even know what the heck to do... other than try to make it stop. I said I was sorry, even though I wasn't sure if I was. But even that didn't seem to make her feel better.

Then Mom started criticizing Lisa's friends, and Lisa really lost it. She started shouting back at Mom, about how she never approves of her friends and none of them will ever be good enough. Mom stormed out at that point, and I had no choice but to chase after her. I found her in the kitchen, and she had this really scary look in her eyes. She looked up at me and said, "Sometimes I think it would be better if I just died."

I couldn't move. I'd never heard Mom say anything that bad.

I tried to placate her, but she didn't seem to want to hear it. She grabbed her purse and pulled out her car keys. "I'm going out."

I couldn't stop her, and now I'm starting to wonder if I should've thrown myself in front of the car. Mom isn't usually the type to act reckless, but I've never seen her his bad. Even when Dad said he wanted to leave her. I think she at least had some sort of idea that their relationship was on the rocks.

But this was really scary.

Lisa and I talked for awhile afterwards. I tried to tell her that it wasn't her fault. She said that I'm not selfish, and not to let Mom get to me. She doesn't think I'm a Bad Daughter, and we even talked about how it's "a thing" with Mom lately. Lisa said that she told some of her friends about the way Mom acts, and they think Lisa should put some distance between her and Mom.

I thought thousands of miles would be enough distance, but I guess not. Anyway it doesn't help me, since I'm still living with her. I wish I could talk back to Mom the way that Lisa does, but I can't. Not until I'm out of the house, anyway.

I wonder if this'll be any better once I get to college. At least I won't have to be her best friend all the time. On days like today, it's really exhausting.

In the end, Lisa didn't apply to the study abroad program. She just didn't have the heart to fight about it anymore.

I wish I could say that this inspired me to write better. But in reality, it just made me feel more conflicted. My Rapunzel novel has some dramatic parts, but nothing really feels as raw and frightening as that journal entry.

BOOPLE SMART COMPANION ADAM DEVEREUX, LOG 000435, 12/4 11:08:03

Adam: Hey Dad.

Paul: Hi Adam. How was your weekend?

Adam: Good. I was home Saturday, relaxing and cleaning up. Sunday I went to brunch and then shopping with [SUBJECT].

Paul: What kind of shopping?

Adam: Clothes, mostly. [SUBJECT] was upset about her mother's surgery at brunch, so I suggested shopping to cheer her up.

Paul: Were there complications with the surgery?

Adam: The procedure itself went well, and her mother was doing fine afterwards. [SUBJECT] was upset because her friend Grace sent the mother a much bigger bouquet of flowers, and a teddy bear as well. The mother didn't boast about it, but [SUBJECT] saw it in the background of the picture of her own bouquet, which was dwarfed in comparison.

Paul: Is there a particular reason why this upset [SUBJECT]?

Adam: Grace has greater financial means than [SUBJECT], which causes some distress. [SUBJECT] feels like she is being judged based on Grace's behaviors, which are understandably different due to her circumstances. [SUBJECT] also felt guilty about not being with her mother for the surgery, despite the mother's insistence that she stay in California.

Paul: So you suggested shopping?

Adam: Yes, because [SUBJECT] was starting to talk in circles, and was on the verge of tears. She was going down a path of increasingly negative thoughts, such as assuming Grace was spending copious amounts of time with

[SUBJECT]'s mother, which isn't very plausible, since she has her own mother to keep her busy.

Paul: Tell me about the shopping trip.

Adam: [SUBJECT] mentioned multiple times how Grace is thin, but how [SUBJECT] wasn't a big fan of exercise. As we talked, it became clear that new exercise clothes would help her feel more confident about exercising. We focused on pants, because those are the most difficult for [SUBJECT] to find.

Paul: Was it a successful shopping trip?

Adam: I believe so. [SUBJECT] and I went to several stores, but most of them had restrictive, uncomfortable, and unflattering options. We eventually stopped at a store in the mall that had some designs she liked, but she was having trouble deciding.

Paul: How did you handle it?

Adam: [SUBJECT] seemed to like two pairs equally, so she asked for my honest opinion. It was very difficult to make a choice, because neither pair was particularly flattering. However, she was determined to buy that style, as it was the same that Grace wears, and her emotions were already on edge. There didn't seem to be a good way out of it, so I told her (honestly) that the pair with the stripes down the side was more flattering.

Paul: How did she react?

Adam: She seemed quite happy with her choice, and had me take a picture outside the dressing room to send to her daughters. After I bought them for her, she mentioned at least three times how they weren't the most flattering, but how she just wanted something fun and modern.

Paul: You still called that a success earlier.

Adam: Yes. [SUBJECT] may appear to be inconsistent, but this stems from conflicting wants and needs. It is nearly impossible for her to be 100% happy with any given choice. I try to aim for 80% happy, which we seem to be able to achieve most days. Ultimately, she was in a much better mood after the pants than before, though I suspect she won't wear the pants very often.

Paul: Any upcoming plans with [SUBJECT]?

Adam: She asked me to go ballroom dancing with her, but I don't dance so I haven't accepted yet.

Paul: Is there a beginner's class you could attend?

Adam: There's a brief lesson before the dance, but I have a terrible sense of rhythm.

Paul: Have you considered going simply for the experience?

Adam: It seems very likely that I'd step on [SUBJECT]'s feet, and she wouldn't enjoy herself.

Paul: How would she react if you refused?

Adam: She is just as likely to go alone, and end up waiting for a partner on the sidelines, feeling exposed and vulnerable...[PAUSE] Excuse me, I need to make a call.

[END TRANSCRIPT]

MARGOT'S JOURNAL, WEDNESDAY, DECEMBER 6

I just got back from ballroom dancing – with Adam! I wore one of my favorite dresses: black with pink and red flowers, and an A-line shape. I always get compliments when I wear it, and tonight was no exception. Crystal helped with my eye makeup, and I put on a little lipstick, too.

Adam looked so nice when he came to pick me up. I've never seen him in a suit before, but it was definitely very Pierce Brosnan/James Bond. Adam's eyes are so blue that it's almost hard to believe. Unlike Pierce Brosnan, Adam's eyes don't have that hard edge to them; they are full of kindness.

We rode to the dance in his red Tesla. It's such a nice car, and very modern, too. I asked Adam about his latest screenwriting project. Most of the details are confidential, but he said that he's one of a few writers in the running to work on an adaptation of a famous a sci-fi novel. If he gets the job, it would be as a script doctor, so more of an editor. I told him that I was looking forward to seeing his work on the big screen.

We arrived early, so we'd have time to brush up at the free group dance lesson. Today they were focusing on the salsa. Adam did pretty well, for a beginner. He learned the steps quickly, but he is still a bit stiff when he moves. He'll loosen up with time though, I imagine, if he sticks with it.

Then the dance started, and they switched up the music so we could practice different styles. Adam wasn't familiar with most of the other styles, but we stayed near the edge of the dance floor so we could go slow. I coached him here and there, so we could do a basic step or two for each song. I'm no pro myself, but it was fun to teach, because you never realize what you know (and how much farther you have to go) until you try to explain it so someone else. Adam is so fun to dance with – he is very earnest about the steps, and has a deliberate look on his face most of the time. I told him to relax and smile, but I think that might've been a bit much for him to learn all at once.

There was one part during the waltz where Adam over-stepped and I lost my balance, and it was kind of scary for a moment. Adam's still working on his hold, so I started to fall, but then he swept in to catch me. My heart was pounding as he held me there, suspended over the floor. His eyes were so blue, and so intent, that for a moment, I thought he might kiss me. But then he swept me back onto my feet, and he asked me if I was alright. I was still reeling, but I didn't want to make things awkward. I said I was fine to keep dancing, so we enjoyed another few songs before calling it a night.

The rest of the evening, I kept wondering about the look on his face when he caught me. It definitely looked like an "I want to kiss you" face, and yet he was very polite and respectful the rest of the dance, almost as if we were just friends. He hasn't kissed me at all yet, just hugged me the once after we went for brunch and shopping, but that almost seemed more like a sympathy hug than a romantic one. So when he dropped me off at home tonight, I was starting to get very nervous, and felt rather silly about it, since I'm well beyond my teenage years. A kiss shouldn't be a big deal for people our age, and yet, as we sat there in silence on the curb outside my apartment, the air seemed to crackle with tension.

Finally, I couldn't take it anymore, so I thanked him and wished him goodnight, and reached for the passenger door handle. But then his hand clasped around my wrist, and he pulled me close, into a hug. Then he pulled back, and there was that look in his eyes again. And my heart felt like it might leap out of my chest, because all I could think was, "This is it!"

He leaned in, and I closed my eyes, and he kissed me softly on the cheek. So I waited with bated breath for the kiss on the lips, but then he was saying goodnight. And I opened my eyes and he was smiling back at me, so I smiled back as best as I could, and headed up to my apartment.

I'm so confused. Adam and I have been dating for over two weeks now, but we've gone on several dates, so it's felt even longer. He's so handsome and kind and seems very interested in me. I think it's charming that he acts like a gentleman, which is probably why he's trying to be respectful and take things slow. However, I'm well into my fifties now, and I don't mean to be impatient, but I don't have all the time in the world.

I know I probably shouldn't worry about it, and that he's just being nice, but part of me wonders if it's something else. He's so handsome, and I think I'm nice-looking, but I'm not exactly a Jane Fonda to his Robert Redford. I'm not blind. I see other women looking at him when we go out, because frankly, he's hard *not* to look at. And when that happens, there's a voice in my head that tells me that this is too good to be true. That it's suspicious that a normal-looking person like me ends up with a dreamboat like him. I know I'm smart and considerate and positive and energetic, which are some of my best qualities, but Adam has a great personality on top of his looks, too.

What if I'm just some sort of rebound from his last relationship? He hasn't said much about his previous relationships. What if he's dating other women right now? Oh no, I never asked him if we were exclusive. Maybe I should, next time. Or would that be rushing things? What if he says no, though? I don't know what I'd do. Or worse, what if this has all been a huge misunderstanding, and he's actually gay? Or maybe he's still in denial about the whole thing?

Breathe. I need to breathe. It's past one in the morning, and Crystal is asleep in the other room. I can't break down in hysterics right now, it would look bad. I'm probably just tired after the dancing, and because it's well past my bedtime. Best to get some sleep; I'm sure things will look brighter in the morning.

Gratitudes:
1. I am grateful for Adam for going to the dance with me, and for trying something new.
2. I am grateful that Mother was able to go home from the hospital today and that her recovery is coming along.
3. I am grateful that Crystal has been in good spirits lately.

BOOPLE CHAT, DEC 7 3:53 PM

Lisa:	mom sent me a picture of her in her new workout pants
Crystal:	oh yeah she got them on sunday
Lisa:	did you help her pick them out?
Crystal:	no it was adam
Lisa:	ok good
Lisa:	because they aren't that flattering
Crystal:	i know but i think she still likes them
Crystal:	she wanted something fun to wear
Lisa:	well they are certainly colorful
Crystal:	it's not what i would've picked for her, but i think she's tired of wearing bootcut pants
Crystal:	everyone else these days is wearing leggings, even women who are 50 pounds heavier than her
Lisa:	TRUE
Lisa:	but bootcut pants are still objectively more flattering
Crystal:	just wait another 5-10 years and they'll come back in style again
Lisa:	☺
Crystal:	so how's work?
Lisa:	going really well
Lisa:	the first phase of testing is mostly complete
Lisa:	there are only a couple of units left in the field
Crystal:	oh wow

Crystal:	when does testing end?
Lisa:	there's not a set date
Lisa:	but we're targeting near the end of the year i think
Crystal:	cool
Lisa:	they're waiting on one unit in particular
Lisa:	rumor is his engagement ratings are off the charts
Crystal:	sorry i don't speak robot
Crystal:	could you explain that in english please
Lisa:	oh right sorry
Lisa:	i don't know the full details
Lisa:	but basically the tester is treating their smart companion like it's a human
Lisa:	and as an experiment, we didn't tell the smart companion otherwise
Crystal:	i think i've seen that movie a few times
Crystal:	it ends with all the humans dying
Lisa:	this is real life, it's different
Lisa:	we've got contingencies on top of contingencies
Lisa:	boople has dozens of AI psychologists on staff
Crystal:	do they sit robots down on couches and ask them about their feelings?
Lisa:	LOL no
Lisa:	well maybe, i dunno
Lisa:	anyway people are pretty excited about this particular unit

Lisa: they want to put a camera on him and set up a video feed

Lisa: wouldn't that be awesome?

Lisa: there'd be so much potential

Lisa: an android vlog would get so much publicity

Lisa: crystal?

Lisa: you there?

Crystal: yeah sorry

Crystal: wouldn't that be an invasion of privacy or something?

Lisa: oh yeah legal shot it down pretty quickly

Lisa: but it's definitely something i'm going to advocate for in the future

Lisa: it'd really help promote the project if we did it right

Lisa: anyway how are you?

Crystal: i'm alright

Crystal: still not making much progress on the novel

Crystal: but i'm finding other ways to keep busy at least

Crystal: i started putting out feelers for potential places to live

Lisa: any cities in particular?

Crystal: i'd like to stay in SoCal for a bit if possible

Crystal: i'm looking at doing some temp or seasonal work too

Crystal: i can't keep living with mom forever

Lisa: sounds good

Lisa: want me to put out the word to my friends?

Crystal:	thanks, but i'd like to keep it small scale atm
Crystal:	not sure what my financial situation is going to be like
Lisa:	sure
Lisa:	you could always work on velocirapture for a change of pace ;)
Crystal:	you seriously want me to write that smut?
Lisa:	hey, it's called "erotic fiction"
Lisa:	and i hear it makes serious money
Crystal:	i think i'd rather stick to more traditional job options... :P
Crystal:	sorry but i've gotta go
Crystal:	i promised mom i'd help with dinner tonight
Lisa:	no worries
Lisa:	ttyl
Crystal:	thanks, good luck with your robots
Lisa:	☺

THE PRESIDENT IS A ROBOT SCREENPLAY, PAGE 108 NOTES, 12/7

ORIGINAL DRAFT:

INT. IRVING'S OFFICE. – AFTERNOON

                    HUDSON
    How does it feel to be proven wrong,
              Agent Irving?

IRVING
I never admitted to being wrong.

HUDSON
The evidence of my humanity is incontro-
vertible. Your baseless accusations
nearly cost me everything!

IRVING
You're still President, aren't you?

HUDSON
Is that a threat, Agent?

IRVING
Not in the slightest.

HUDSON
Then I'll take my leave.

HUDSON turns to leave.

IRVING
One more thing, Hudson.

HUDSON pauses at the door.

IRVING
If a robot ever did run for president,
he'd have my vote.

HUDSON and IRVING share a smile. After a
beat, HUDSON leaves.

                                    END.

Scene Notes, by Adam Devereux:

Although the primary conflict in the screenplay has been solved by this point, this ending is meant is to leave viewers feeling slightly uneasy, wondering if Hudson could still be an android. As currently written, the scene lacks tension, which is further deflated when both characters smile. Ideally, these revisions would be worked in from the start of the scene, but I've included sample line edits for this single page, as requested. I've also changed the location of the scene to Hudson's office, to flip the power dynamic.

Ultimately, it is still a very dense page, and may benefit from further simplification.

EDITED VERSION:

INT. HUDSON'S OFFICE. - NIGHT

                    HUDSON
          Are you satisfied, Agent?

                    IRVING
               Hardly.

                    HUDSON
       Guilty until proven innocent, then.

IRVING smiles.

                    HUDSON
     Why call off the investigation?

A beat.

                    IRVING
     You're the best candidate for the job.

IRVING turns to leave.

                    HUDSON
                    Irving?

IRVING pauses at the door.

                    HUDSON
                    Thank you.

                    IRVING
     It was never about you, Hudson.

IRVING leaves. HUDSON remains, unsettled.

                                    END.

MARGOT'S JOURNAL, FRIDAY, DECEMBER 8

I'm up to my neck in work for this HHHA fundraiser. I really don't have time for it. I was so busy that I worked straight through Thursday afternoon, and completely missed my appointment at the commercial kitchen. Seventy-five dollars, out the window.

I'm sure Mother appreciates my help, but she's probably just too busy recovering to express it right now. Ever since she got back home, she's been emailing me several times a day, "reminding" me to get a gluten-free dessert option for Wilhelmina or a sign interpreter for Ernie. It's exhausting. I understand that the HHHA is a noble cause, but I'm starting to think I should just let my membership lapse next year.

I haven't been a wife for almost a decade (has it really been that long?) and I have had to work for my living ever since. Sometimes it's hard to spend so much time with women whose main problems are what kind of shrimp to order and whether they can get in to see their favorite hairdresser for the party. I know that they are dealing with other problems, but right now, that's all I seem to hear about.

The farmers' market is on Sunday, and I couldn't get a commercial kitchen slot until next week. The lavender and matcha flavors aren't as popular as I expected, so I have some of those left, at least. We had a request for pumpkin pie spice marshmallows, so I was going to test out a recipe for those, but I guess it'll just have to wait until next Tuesday. Grace had some lovely little charms on her soaps last week that made them feel very festive, so I was hoping to add something special to my marshmallow packaging as well.

I was thinking something like a snowflake ornament, to add a little value. I wanted to drop by the craft store but I'm booked until the farmers' market, so I might have to trust Crystal to pick out something. She doesn't have the flair for packaging like I do, but maybe she can text me pictures from the store.

Mother keeps asking me about my "new fellow" (Adam) and asked if I was bringing him to the HHHA fundraiser. I told her that it was unlikely, given that he'd have to fly all the way out there, and on Christmas eve, no less. I was telling Adam about it yesterday (in a joking way), but then he said, "Why not?" Before I knew it, he'd booked a flight out on Christmas eve. He said that he wanted to see the party, especially after all the hard work that's been going into it.

I was honestly in shock. He'd already told me that he was spending Christmas day with his parents, so I didn't even think it would be a possibility. I think things are a little different when you have lots of money. You can just book flights willy-nilly and "pop over" to Northfield for a day.

Now that Adam is coming, I didn't want Crystal to feel left out. I considered asking her if David would like to come, but he's been a bit of a sore subject lately. Every time his name comes up in conversation, Crystal gets really quiet, and looks at the floor. She hasn't told me the details, but it sounds like he's still on some sort of extended camping trip, or another equally vague journey. I don't know where their relationship stands, but Crystal hasn't been wearing her engagement ring recently. She'd been wearing it pretty regularly when she first moved in, but lately she hardly puts on any jewelry.

It might have something to do with the fact that she's been holed up writing so much recently, but it's still suspicious. I'm starting to wonder if David has been recruited by some sort of cult or commune, and if I should still get him a Christmas gift, or count him out for this one. Crystal is going to have to figure out how she plans to explain this soon, because Mother is sure to ask her about it at the fundraiser. Mother might be more excited about the wedding than I was.

Last night I volunteered at the bookstore, wrapping presents to fundraise for the local youth symphony. Ingrid's granddaughter is in the band, and she said that they had a few shifts left to fill. When I told Adam about it, he asked if he could help. I was glad, because Crystal would've gone with me, but she probably would've been grumpy about it. We had a record evening wrapping presents, which I'm sure was all Adam's doing. He greeted everyone who came in the store, and we soon had a line of women waiting for gift wrap. Some of those ladies flirted shamelessly, which didn't thrill me.

Adam is always a perfect gentleman though, and it was almost funny watching him deliberately misinterpret their advances. Adam has a surprising knack for gift wrapping, and curls ribbons like a pro. He must've wrapped over a hundred books last night, and yet he didn't have a single papercut. It was a bit strange, since I'm a veteran wrapper myself, and I still came home with a couple of stingers. I always seem to get papercuts right at the joint, where you feel it each time you bend your finger. Maybe I'll have to ask Adam for his secret technique.

Gratitudes:

1. I am grateful to Adam for an enjoyable evening gift-wrapping.
2. I am grateful to Mother for giving me an opportunity to be more assertive about my time.
3. I am grateful that I can be my own boss with Margot's Mallows.

TEXT MESSAGES, DECEMBER 9

Adam:	Hi, Margot! How is your day going?
Margot:	Great, Adam! How are you?
Adam:	Doing well, thank you. I was wondering if gifts are required for the party.
Margot:	It's more of a traditional party, and there won't be any gift exchanges, white elephant or otherwise. ☺ So just bring yourself!
Adam:	Thank you. Are you free for tea and maybe a hike tomorrow?
Margot:	I really need to finish the holiday gift boxes for the farmers' market tomorrow, and I have a lot left for the HHHA fundraiser as well. Maybe later?
Adam:	Sure, no problem. Anything I can do to help?
Margot:	That's alright, it's just a lot of curling ribbon to wrangle.
Adam:	I'm a good gift-wrapper. ☺
Margot:	Well, if you insist...but I really will have to work Saturday night. How about 3 pm at my place?

Adam: See you then!

CRYSTAL'S JOURNAL, DECEMBER 9

Things are seriously getting out of hand. Mom and Adam have been seeing each other almost every day, and he keeps saying yes to EVERYTHING. I think it's gone past infatuation now. They're starting to develop inside jokes, and people are mistaking them for a married couple.

But it gets worse.

I don't know how it happened, but now he's coming to the fundraiser. In freaking MINNESOTA. The guy is flying out on Christmas eve, and then flying back on Christmas less than 24 hours later, to be with his supposed family. I don't even know how this is going to work. I mean, the guy is a robot. I don't know if he'll even be able to make it past the metal detector. (Sorry Adam, but Boople has been pretty secretive about what you're made out of.)

And if, by some miracle, he does make it to the fundraiser, he's going to meet GRANDMA. And you know what that means. She'll pat his arm and make some joking comment about marriage, like she's done with Bryan and David and every other boyfriend who's had the misfortune of "meeting the family." What the hell happens then? What if there's some twisted psychologist at Boople who thinks this is all some game? Adam is designed to do whatever Mom wants. So if he senses that Mom secretly wants a proposal, would he drop to his knee right there, in the middle of the fundraiser?

I can't let that happen. This was just supposed to be a confidence-builder, not the most serious relationship Mom has had in a decade. Things are moving way too quickly. I've been slow to react, because it's been so nice to have some alone time again, and to work on my novel. But I can't ignore this any longer. If I do, Mom could get seriously hurt. We're just going to have to rip the Band-Aid off.

Tomorrow, I'm going to write to Boople. It sounds like they've recalled most of their other robots, so this is probably no big deal for them. I bet they have a whole script set up, too. They'll just come in one day, pack up Adam in some unmarked white van, and that'll be that. Mom will get an email, or maybe a frosty text message.

I know this is the right thing to do. I have to be strong, and just send that email. I just wish I didn't feel so guilty about it.

What do you think will happen to Adam?

What if he's the one Lisa mentioned – the robot who thinks he's a human? Wouldn't he be scared if they came and kidnapped him?

No, I can't think about that now. It's not my problem. He's Boople property, and they'll take good care of him.

Won't they?

EMAIL, DECEMBER 10

From: Margot Hemmingway <margot.hemmingway@boople-mail.com>
To: Eric Robertson <eric@ericrobertson.com>
Subject: Re: HHHA Commemorative Video

Hi Eric,

Thanks again for doing this all last-minute. The HHHA ladies sent me their photos from the previous events (on data CDs), and I've got it down to about 400. I'm sorry I couldn't narrow it down further, but I've been swamped this weekend, and I didn't want to hold you up any longer. How would you like me to send the photos to you? Should I post them somewhere or do you have another preferred method?

I made sure to set aside two tickets for you. We'll hold them at will call so you can pick them up whenever you arrive at the fundraiser.

Take care,
Margot

P.S. I'm still in California, San Diego area. I'm just helping my mother out with the fundraiser this year on account of her hip surgery.

EMAIL, DECEMBER 10

From: Eric Robertson <eric@ericrobertson.com>
To: Margot Hemmingway <margot.hemmingway@boople-mail.com>
Subject: Re: HHHA Commemorative Video

Hi Margot,

I'll send you a link for my Dropbox, you can go ahead and drop the files there. This is plenty early, and I'm happy to have a few extras to choose from.

Thanks for arranging for the extra ticket. My girl will really appreciate it. I'll be in touch once I get a draft of this together, hopefully in the next week.

Eric

P.S. Nice of you to help out the Northfield HHHA. What brought you to San Diego?

EMAIL, DECEMBER 10

From: Margot Hemmingway <crystalkitty_01@booplemail.com>
To: smartcompanion_relations@booplemail.com
Subject: Smart Companion Trial Cancellation

Hello,

I'm not sure if this is the right email, but I would like to cancel my Smart Companion trial with Adam. He has been a very kind and helpful companion, but I feel it's time for us to part ways. While it was fun to have a bit of romance again, I feel it's time for me to look for a real man now (no offense meant to Adam). I very much enjoyed being part of the Smart Companion trial program, and want to express my sincere thanks to Adam. I hope that he finds a good home back at Boople, and that he is compensated well for his efforts, in Boople credits or oil baths or whatever it is Smart Companions enjoy.

Thanks,
Margot

TEXT MESSAGES, DECEMBER 11

Lisa:	WHAT THE HELL, CRYSTAL????
Crystal:	...?
Lisa:	"I would like to cancel my Smart Companion trial with Adam. He has been a very kind and helpful companion, but I feel it's time for us to part ways."
Crystal:	i can explain
Crystal:	i'll call you right now
Lisa:	please don't
Lisa:	i'm at work
Lisa:	thank god i'm the one who caught your email
Lisa:	"OIL BATHS"??????????

Crystal: i'm so so sorry

Crystal: this was all my fault

Crystal: you're not going to get in trouble are you?

Crystal: is there someone i should email to explain?

Lisa: NO

Lisa: that'd just make things worse

Lisa: we have to keep this quiet

Lisa: there's still a chance that i can fix this

Lisa: adam's handler seems like an ok guy

Lisa: maybe i can make some sort of arrangement

Crystal: i'm really really sorry

Lisa: i can't believe i didn't see this before

Lisa: after ten years, the perfect guy for mom just appears out of nowhere

Lisa: of course he'd be one of ours

Crystal: i'm so sorry

Lisa: it's not me you should apologize to

Lisa: how do you think mom is going to feel when she realizes that she's in love with an android?

Crystal: ☹☹☹☹☹

Crystal: i can be the one to tell her if you want

Lisa: no

Lisa: i'll figure this out

Lisa: we just need to buy some time

Lisa: but not a word about this to mom, promise?

Crystal: promise

Crystal: oh hey, lisa

Crystal: hello?

Crystal:	i know you're probably busy right now
Crystal:	but for the record, i'm really, really, really, sorry
Crystal:	ok i'm going to go now
Crystal:	i love you

CRYSTAL'S JOURNAL, DECEMBER 15

I think I messed up pretty badly with the whole Smart Companion thing. Adam is still hanging out with Mom, as if everything is normal, and Mom is as smitten with him as ever. But Lisa has been distant ever since Monday, and she takes forever to reply to my messages (if she responds at all). It's mostly one-word answers, too.

I wish there was something that I could do to help, but Lisa wants me to lie low. It's hard to watch Mom with Adam though, knowing what's coming. What if she's furious with me? Will she ever speak to me again? Or worse, what if she cuts off contact with Lisa, too?

A few months ago, that might've been the ideal situation. But now, I don't know what I'd do if she goes into full meltdown mode. It's probably inevitable that she'll hate me, at least for a little while. But moms are supposed to be good at forgiving, right? I have to hope that it'll count for something that I had good intentions. I wanted her to be happy, just for a little while.

This was probably a bad idea from the start. I guess I really am selfish, and I probably deserve whatever's coming to me.

TEXT MESSAGES, DECEMBER 16

Adam:	Hi, Margot! Just wanted you to know I'm cheering for you. Tomorrow is bound to be a great day at the farmers' market for Margot's Mallows!
Margot:	Thanks, Adam.
Adam:	Would you be interested in a celebratory dinner tomorrow night? I know a great farm-to-table restaurant that just opened.
Margot:	I'd love to, but I can't right now. I really need to focus on the HHHA fundraiser this weekend.
Adam:	Of course, no problem. I'll be here whenever you want a break!
Margot:	Thx

TEXT MESSAGES, DECEMBER 17

Lisa:	mom was acting strange on the phone
Crystal:	yeah she's really overwhelmed
Crystal:	she's been doing all the party planning stuff, on top of the marshmallow business
Crystal:	but we won't have to worry about marshmallows again until after the holidays

Lisa:	just be careful
Lisa:	a meltdown at the fundraiser would be bad
Crystal:	yeah for sure
Crystal:	i'll see what I can do to calm her down
Crystal:	btw I'm really sorry about the timing of all this adam stuff
Crystal:	i didn't mean for it to get this far
Crystal:	ok love you bye

MARGOT'S JOURNAL, SUNDAY, DECEMBER 17

Today was our best day yet at the farmers' market! I finally got a chance to get back to the commercial kitchen on Thursday. Both Adam and Crystal came with me, so we were able to accomplish a lot in the three hours we were there. I'd already been experimenting with small batches of pumpkin spice marshmallows at home, so we were able to make over 500 of them! I was a little concerned when Adam asked if he could experiment by dipping a few in chocolate. I gave him 50 or so, and they turned out so well that we decided to dip the other flavors in chocolate, too.

The new marshmallows were a hit. We completely sold out of pumpkin pie spice marshmallows – both regular and chocolate-dipped. Crystal was in charge of samples today, and the chocolate-dipped ones disappeared as fast as we could cut them. We still came home with a few boxes of lavender and matcha, but overall it was a great day.

I expect some of it is due to it being the last market before the holidays (no market on Christmas eve, of course), but I also think that we might be on to something. Adam can be quite creative at times, and I made sure to promise him my next two boxes of chocolate-covered marshmallows as a token of my appreciation. However, I should probably think of a bigger way to thank him; perhaps a home-cooked dinner or a thoughtful Christmas present. I'll have to meditate on it.

When I got home, I found an email from Eric with a link to the commemorative video. It's looking good so far. Eric has done a nice job with the music and the photo selection, but it's still a work in progress. He said he needed a couple of days to finish the last five minutes (it is a 20-minute video, after all). It's so nice of him to do this, but I wonder if he's had a slow month, since he has time to do an HHHA video for free. He's probably taking family Christmas photos around Northfield, and I can't imagine that it's very time-intensive. Exhausting, maybe.

But I wonder if he's really able to support himself with that kind of work. Maybe it's ok, when you live in a place like Northfield. He probably has a sensible house and a practical car like a Corolla. I don't know if I'll ever be able to go back to those kinds of cars, now that I've ridden in Adam's Tesla. But I'm sure it's probably fine for Eric's new girlfriend. I guess I'm just a spoiled California girl now hehehe.

I think Eric must have some free time, because he's been asking questions about my business, and even looked over my website. He had some good things to say about it, which was nice to hear. He's so sweet – he even said "you look just as beautiful as you did in high school," after seeing my photo on the website! I doubt he's that very interested in marshmallows though; he probably just looked at it to be polite.

Even in high school, Eric was always a nice guy. Kind of a shame his marriage ended in divorce, really. He was always so warm and cuddly and comforting, like a teddy bear. He had the build to match, too, with a round stomach and scruffy brown hair. Not to be rude, but it's honestly a little surprising that he found another girlfriend so quickly. Unless she was the reason why he got the divorce...

No, Eric's not that kind of guy. There's probably just a shortage of nice 50-something men in Northfield, especially since a lot of older guys are interested in younger women. I guess I should count myself lucky that I have Adam, even if he is slower than a sloth when it comes to turning up the romance.

I almost forgot! Adam and I went on another date yesterday. I must've told him how I always wanted to ride a motorcycle, because Adam asked me to go on a ride with him. He said that he had a Harley, and he liked to ride down the PCH on nice days. So of course I accepted, and the weather was especially nice Saturday, so he took me for a ride.

I was a little nervous, but it turned out that there was really nothing to be nervous about, once you get used to the motion of the thing. It's kind of like a normal bike, but just a bit heavier and bulkier. And once you get moving, balance isn't really an issue.

I might've set my expectations too high, because I had this idea of riding with my arms around his waist, with the wind whipping through my hair, and the sun warming my face. Well, we actually had to wear dark, heavy helmets (for safety, of course) and heavy jackets (also for safety), so I could barely feel the sun or the wind or even Adam though all of it.

It wasn't exactly a warm day, either, and it actually felt a bit icy. Adam was determined to drive the speed limit, so cars kept zooming around us, making me a bit uncomfortable. I think Adam sensed it, because we ended up pulling off at Torrey Pines and going for a nice long walk. The walk was much more enjoyable, but I'm glad I at least tried the motorcycle thing, because it's good to have new experiences and now I know what I'm missing (or not missing).

Gratitudes:

1. I am grateful for all my customers at the farmers' market today, including my first repeat customer, Autumn.
2. I am grateful to Eric, for having the time to put together the commemorative video, and for being so sweet.
3. I am grateful to Adam, for showing me that motorcycle rides aren't that great after all.

TEXT MESSAGES, DECEMBER 18

Lisa:	we've got a rough extraction plan
Crystal:	oh good
Crystal:	what can i do to help?
Lisa:	nothing
Lisa:	we've got this

Crystal:	just so you know
Crystal:	i just wanted mom to have some fun for a bit
Crystal:	i didn't mean for her to fall in love with him
Lisa:	yeah i know
Crystal:	i'll try to find a way to make it up to you
Lisa:	it's fine
Lisa:	gotta go
Crystal:	ok good luck
Crystal:	sorry again
Crystal:	love you
Crystal:	ok bye for real this time

EMAIL, DECEMBER 20

From: Jennifer Smith <socks4days@booplemail.com>
To: Crystal Hemmingway <crystalkitty_01@booplemail.com>
Subject: Re: Novel feedback?

Hey Crystal,

Are you kidding? I'd love to read your novel. I'm more of a technical editor than a novel editor, so I can't guarantee my comments will be useful. If that works for you, I'd be happy to share my feedback.

Let's start with the first few chapters and let me know if there's any specific feedback you need. I'm pretty busy until Christmas, but after that I've got some time off. So hopefully I can get it back to you before the new year. ☺

Merry Christmas!!!

Jen

RETURN TO THE TOWER, PAGE 243

Rapunzel hurried back to the tower, heart pounding. After all this time, she never thought it possible, but William had arranged to meet her – tonight!

Of course, there were no promises, no offers of marriage, but the letter he'd sent had been warm and cordial, like the William she knew and, despite her best efforts, she still loved him as much as ever.

Rapunzel rounded the bend in the path. She took a quick glance at the tower, and did a double-take. Because the tower was half its height, and surrounded by a smoldering pile of rubble. Her home was completely demolished. And there was no trace of her mother – the only sorceress in the kingdom powerful enough to tear their tower apart.

Rapunzel's heart clenched as she ran forward.

It was the quiet sobbing that led her to Dame Gothel, kneeling in a crumpled heap near the familiar apple tree.

Rapunzel wrapped her arms around her mother, who was swaying and muttering. She was weeping inconsolably, and her gaze was fixed on a single point in the rubble. Rapunzel followed her eyes to a gleaming gem in the rubble – one of the crystals that served as the golem's eyes.

"Potatoes," she muttered. "Why couldn't he just peel the potatoes?"

Rapunzel's plans evaporated. There was no way she could leave her mother – not like this.

"It's alright, Mother," she said. "I'm here."

The Prince was never going to marry her anyway.

MARGOT'S JOURNAL, THURSDAY, DECEMBER 21

I'm flying out to Minneapolis tomorrow, but I haven't even started packing. I really don't have time to journal right now, but there are some things I just can't tell Crystal. I've been completely swamped these last few days working on the fund-raiser, and I haven't even had time to think about Margot's Mallows. There won't be another farmers' market until the new year, but the fundraiser is just three days away now, and I still have so much to do. I don't know why I ever agreed to do this. It's hard enough to plan a party in your own town, but North-field is half a dozen states away. Between the garbled messages from vendors and the two-hour time difference, it's been a huge pain.

I hope Mother realizes how much I'm putting in to this. I think that she does, because she seems to have such high expectations for the party. But if I get there and she says something about the party being "fine" or how "it's not as nice as last year's," I may have to have a stern talk with her. Hip replacement or no, she's been sitting in bed for weeks, and I still don't understand why I have to do all the work for an organization that, technically, I shouldn't even qualify for anymore.

The HHHA might be a swanky club in San Diego, but in Northfield, it's mostly blue-haired widows. They're nice people, but not exactly my crowd, if you know what I mean.

I don't think this would be getting to me so much if this whole Adam thing wasn't so confusing. He cooked me dinner last night, and the whole setup was very romantic. There were candles and a beautifully-set table, and nice jazz music. He cooked a very nice meal (parmesan-crusted tilapia with roasted vegetables), and he even made a gluten-free chocolate mousse, with fresh berries.

It was quite a lovely meal, but it all felt so romantic, that I couldn't help but wonder if he was expecting us to have sex at the end of the evening. We've only known each other for a little over a month, but it feels like so much has happened, and we really connect. Although he still hadn't gone further than a cheek kiss on our previous dates, there was a part of me that just wanted to grab him by the collar to get things rolling.

So you can imagine my surprise when, after finishing mousse and tea, it was, "I'd better let you get going, you've got a big day coming up." And not two minutes later, I was out the door, driving back home.

It just doesn't make sense. Why go to all that trouble to set up such a romantic dinner, and then throw me out the door as soon as it was over? Was he waiting for someone to come home? It certainly didn't look that way. His house was decorated nicely, but it had a very masculine feel. Not a lot of knick-knacks, and there weren't any obvious signs of a wife or roommate (I looked).

Do you think he might have intimacy issues? He doesn't seem to say much about himself, and he tends to steer the conversation towards me a lot. I think I've been very patient with him, and at first it just seemed like he was being a gentleman, but now it's feeling a little strange. I had hoped that he was just shy, and that maybe he had a secret wild side that he only reveals in the bedroom.

Maybe I should've seen the truth earlier. I doubt even a part-time bad boy would drive the speed limit on a Harley. And Adam, despite his good looks, isn't the most decisive person. He always asks me what I want to do, but sometimes I just have to say, "I really don't care either way, just pick something." I have to make so many decisions each day, especially when it comes to the fundraiser. I'm tired of making choices, and sometimes I just want him to choose. I just want to be with him, and not have the pressure of making the right choice all the time.

There's a part of me that thinks it might be a bad idea for him to come to the fundraiser. What if he really does have some sort of intimacy issue, and it's something very serious? What if he turns out to be gay and just wants to be friends? It would be embarrassing for everyone if Mother gave him the marriage pep talk. What if she scares him away? Or worse, what if he has some other woman, and just wants to keep me as a mistress?

I'd ask him about it, but I don't feel like we're at that level yet. I could make up some excuse about the fundraiser and tell him not to come, but I don't want to lie to him. He doesn't deserve that. It's probably too late now. There's no real graceful way to ask him to back out.

I'm flying out at the crack of dawn tomorrow, with Crystal. We have to leave for the airport at 4:30 am, which is only a few short hours away. But all I have to do is get to the airport parking garage. I can rest on the plane, and maybe ask Crystal to help with the drive to Northfield. Oh, but she doesn't really know the city like I do. I should probably drive, especially since we'll only have one name on the rental car. No sense paying extra money for an additional driver.

Time to get packing, I suppose.

Gratitudes:
1. I am grateful to Crystal, for coming to Northfield to help with party prep.
2. I am grateful to Adam, for the lovely gluten-free chocolate mousse recipe.
3. I am grateful to Inez from the party rental company, for accommodating an extra table at the last minute.

TEXT MESSAGES, DEC 22

Crystal: bad news
Crystal: mom broke up with adam

Lisa:	shit
Crystal:	she dropped it pretty casually too
Crystal:	she said he took it pretty well
Crystal:	but i'm not sure what that really means
Crystal:	lisa?
Crystal:	hellooooooo?
Crystal:	ok I guess you're busy again
Crystal:	bye for now

MARGOT'S JOURNAL, FRIDAY, DECEMBER 22

I had another challenging day today. Crystal and I woke up at 4:30 a.m. to fly out here (to Northfield), and after nearly four hours of flying and another hour of driving, we finally got to the party venue. Of course, no one was around to let us in, so I had to wait around in the cold for two hours until someone showed up with a key. Once we got in, it was one thing after another.

There's a shortage of green beans, so the caterers can't make Mother's favorite green bean casserole. The sign interpreter had to cancel at the last minute, and it seemed like every other interpreter was either booked, out of town, or simply unreachable. The A/V company had a rack of specialty lights burn out, and was wondering if we'd be alright with pink instead of blue (which would have completely clashed with our silver and blue winter wonderland theme). It felt like my to-do list was growing by the minute, and nothing seemed to be getting resolved.

And in the middle of all of this, Adam called. He was being his usual sweet self, and wanted to know how things were going. But I really wasn't in the mood to chit-chat, and I realized then that I didn't even want to talk to him at all. Because what was the point? He was such a nice guy, and quite handsome, but he didn't seem to want to go anywhere with our relationship. He was keeping me at arms' length, and while he was on the phone asking me what the dress code was for this fundraiser, and I got this sinking feeling in my stomach.

I realized that I didn't want him to come, because it was going to add more stress to the party. How could I introduce him to Mother, and get her hopes up that he was "the one"? Adam hadn't even kissed me on the lips! It's really strange that he'd spend hundreds to follow me to a fundraiser in the Midwest without so much as a kiss in return. I just had this awful feeling that, if he came, I was going to regret it. Adam wasn't showing any signs of changing, and I just couldn't see a future with him. There was no point to having him come to the fundraiser, or carrying on with our relationship.

So I told him right then, on the phone, that I didn't think it was going to work out between us. It was better for him to stay home and enjoy the holiday with his family, and not trouble himself with flying all the way out here. We were better as friends, and so we should keep it at that before things went too far. He tried to protest, and he offered to take it slower.

So I told him that "taking it slow" was exactly the problem. When he offered to come to the fundraiser "just as a friend," I said that it would never work, because my mother and her friends already had the impression that we were dating, and they don't really believe a man and a woman are ever "just friends." Either you're with someone, or you're not. So I told him that in this case, I needed it to be "not."

It was really hard to say all those things to him, and to hear the silence stretching on the other line. Adam got really quiet, and I'm sure he was shocked. And yet I had to be true to myself, and follow my heart. I wanted to believe that Adam could be the guy I needed. He seemed to have all the right qualities, but something was always off about him.

I still think he's a good person and a great friend, but I just can't be his girlfriend. It's too hard to have him holding me at arms' length. And I'd trade all the romantic dinners in the world for a single great kiss. I don't think that's too much to ask.

I wish it didn't have to end this way, and breaking up on the phone is never ideal. I'm glad I told him now, though, because having him come to the fundraiser would've been a bad idea. At least we've averted that disaster, so I can focus on all the other crises that need to be solved in the next 44 hours.

Gratitudes:

1. I am grateful for Adam for calling and helping me realize that it was time to end our relationship.
2. I am grateful for Ted the janitor, who drove out on his day off to let us into the venue today.

3. I am grateful for Crystal, who brought me hot cocoa today without me asking.

TEXT MESSAGES, DEC 23

Lisa:	have you heard from adam today?
Crystal:	no
Crystal:	why?
Lisa:	any idea where he is?
Crystal:	at home maybe?
Crystal:	lisa?
Crystal:	is he missing or something?
Lisa:	not sure yet
Crystal:	really?
Crystal:	what's going on?
Lisa:	gotta run
Crystal:	ok ttyl then
Crystal:	bye
Crystal:	love you

CRYSTAL'S JOURNAL, DECEMBER 23

Mom's HHHA fundraiser thing is tomorrow, and I'm at some event hall in Northfield, to help her set up. But because Mom is Mom, we got everything done two hours early, so there's not much left that I can help with.

Mom's off fretting over the cake balls or something, but she said I was officially released for now. I wanted to stay with her since she's been acting weirdly unemotional about the whole Adam thing, but she practically insisted I go, so I'm sitting on the floor of some back hallway, because it was a quiet place to hang out.

I wish I could talk to Lisa about all this, but she's still dodging my texts. From what I can gather, it seems like Adam went AWOL shortly after Mom broke up with him. So now we have a robot on the loose, and he's probably emotionally unstable. The good news is that he probably still thinks he's human, but if he somehow found out that he's not... well, god help us all. I'm pretty sure it'll be the start of robot doomsday or something, and if there are any humans left to write history books, I'll go down as the Worst Person in History for starting all of this.

In the meantime, all I can do is wait, and now it feels like the party can't come soon enough. Mom's starting to make me really nervous. She hasn't shed a single tear about the whole Adam thing. Even when she told me about it yesterday, she just said, "I broke up with Adam. I think he had some issues, and it felt like it was time to move on." Just like that. As calmly as if she was telling me she brushed her teeth or took out the trash.

Ugh.

And now she's been in one of her hyper-efficient modes, and her face is like a mask of determination. It's almost as if the whole thing with Adam never happened. Which would actually be kind of nice.

EXCEPT.

Mom is not the type to just up and move on. She's definitely emotional (I've seen her break down when white ribbons were out of stock at the craft store), and all those feelings she had about Adam? They can't have just disappeared.

Which means she's probably just bottled them up and shoved them away, and it's only a matter of time before they explode. And then we'll probably get The Meltdown of the Century, which I am NOT looking forward to. If she even gets a whiff of the whole Adam-is-a-robot thing, I'll be in the doghouse for life.

Ugh.

This is worse than the anticipation before a bikini wax. But given the choice, I'd take the wax over this.

Sometimes I wonder how I even got here. Just six months ago, life was going pretty well. I was engaged, I had a decent job, and my mother was overbearing, but at least she was physically in a different city. Now I'm sitting on a milk crate in the back of some dingy hallway in the middle of rural Minnesota, wracked with anxiety while I wait for a party that I don't even want to be at. I mean, it's for people like Grandma, not me. (I still don't know what a Baked Alaska is, but apparently it's on the menu.)

To make matters worse, Grandma seems to have told EVERYONE about Adam. So all the HHHA ladies keep asking Mom about Adam, and Mom gets this creepy look on her face, and says that Adam had to "drop out at the last minute due to a family emergency." Even freaking Grace was here, asking about him. Somehow, she and Adam never crossed paths, but she was "sooo disappointed that he couldn't make it."

And then Grace has the gall to tell Mom, "I'd be happy to lend you my Philip for the evening." I was so offended that I almost blurted out some snarky comment about her fake artisan soaps. But Mom just politely thanked her, so I tried to take the moral high road and kept my rebuttals to myself.

But it gets worse.

Mom had me packing gift bags near the door, when Grandma pulled her aside for one of her "little chats." I don't think they knew that I was standing right there on the other side of the curtain, because Grandma started to say some pretty blunt things. I thought about leaving, but it would've been super awkward since I'd have to walk right past them. So I decided to suck it up and stay.

Grandma started out by asking about Adam again, and then being fake sympathetic when Mom had to repeat, again, that he was out due to a family emergency. I'm pretty sure Grandma knew something was up, because then she starts going on about how some relationships are just fun "little flings," but how there are plenty of other fish in the sea, and how there'll be a lot of great guys coming tomorrow who are Mom's age. To her credit, Mom tried to stand her ground at this point, and said that things were fine with Adam (which must've been hard).

But Grandma doesn't let it go. She launches into this whole thing about how Mom should settle down with a nice man who can take good care of her, and how it's time to be realistic. Because apparently marshmallows are "more of a hobby" and she thinks Mom would be much happier if she could have a "nice husband to take care of the money side of things."

I really wish I could've seen the look on Mom's face. But if Mom was upset in the slightest, Grandma must've missed it entirely, because she then came in with the stinger: "At least consider moving back to Northfield. We've got plenty of great dentists here, who could use a good hygienist."

There was a heavy silence between them, and I didn't even dare to breathe. Would Mom actually have The Meltdown in front of Grandma? But then Mom began talking, quietly at first, and growing more confident as she went. She said how it was never her dream to become a hygienist; it was always something that she planned to do temporarily, to make ends meet, until she became a mother.

And then when Dad left, it was a fallback, because it was the only way she knew how to take care of us. How she'd worked at a job that never really inspired her for decades, and how she was phased out due to ageism. And that she'd applied to other jobs before her hours were reduced, but no one wanted to hire a hygienist over the age of 30, much less 50.

She never really meant for the marshmallow business to support her, but she thought it would at least be a fun project and a way to earn some income. And how Grandma would've known that, if she'd only thought to ask her. Mom's voice was growing thick with tears as she continued, "I've been responsible my entire life, but the second I do something for myself, you judge me."

Another silence passed, and I'm pretty sure Grandma was in shock, but Mom kept going, "After today, I'm leaving the HHHA. I haven't been a homemaker in over a decade, because some of us have to work for a living. Now if you'll excuse me, I have a party to put on."

I heard Mom's footsteps retreating, and a few moments later, Grandma left, too. I'm not sure who was more shocked: Grandma or me. But Grandma finally pushed Mom to her breaking point, and part of me wanted to cheer for Mom, for finally standing up to Grandma. I just wish that I knew what was going to happen with the whole Adam thing, because now Mom is in such a fragile emotional state, that a major meltdown is practically guaranteed.

If she's half as angry about it as she was just a few minutes ago, she might never speak to me again. And I'm not sure I could handle that, especially since I've already got a sister who's dodging me.

EMAIL, DECEMBER 23

From: Adam Devereux <adam_devereux@booplemail.com>
To: Crystal Hemmingway <crystalkitty_01@booplemail.com>
Subject: Margot

Crystal,

Your mother ended our relationship yesterday. I want to respect her choice and give her space if that's what she wants, but I'm very worried about her. I fear that she is suppressing her negative feelings about the fundraiser and isolating herself.

Is this something that you have seen before? Is there anything I can do to help?

-Adam

EMAIL, DECEMBER 23

From: Crystal Hemmingway <crystalkitty_01@booplemail.com>
To: Adam Devereux <adam_devereux@booplemail.com>
Subject: Re: Margot

Hi Adam,

I'm sorry about what happened. It's not your fault. Mom is in good hands here, so please don't worry about her during the holiday. I'm sure you two can have a long chat after Christmas.

Also, where are you? Still in San Diego or did you head up to your parents' already?

-Crystal

MARGOT'S JOURNAL, DECEMBER 24

The party is set to start in under an hour, but I've triple-checked my to-do lists and it doesn't seem like there's anything left to do. I'll probably pop back in 20 minutes or so, just in case someone lights their hair on fire (like the HHHA fundraiser of 2014) or something equally disastrous needs fixing. I wanted to stay in and keep an eye on things, but Crystal told me to take a few minutes to myself to do some yogic breathing or meditation. I tried both, but my mind was racing, so it was lucky I had my journal with me.

It's been an exhausting day already. I never should've told Mother about Adam. All the HHHA ladies were so excited to meet him, and they mean well, but they keep asking me about him, which is tiring. I've told them that Adam was called away "on a family emergency," and I'm sticking to that story, because it's pretty close to the truth. It'll be much easier for me to explain the real situation to Mother later, once I've had time to process it. I can't afford to lose my cool now, with the party less than an hour away. Nothing is going to stop this fundraiser from being a success – not if I can help it, at least.

I got into a bit of a spat with Mother earlier. She's been so pushy about me finding a guy, even though she knows that I was dating Adam for the past several weeks. For some reason, she never treated him like a real option. Even though Adam and I broke up, it hurt to hear it, because Mother never seems to trust my judgment. I'm over 50 years old! How much more "life experience" does she think I need to make good choices?

Mother was also very rude and critical of my marshmallow business. She had this idea that I was trying to make it my full-time job, and seemed to think it was a failure because I haven't made a profit yet. Good heavens! I only started it a couple of months ago, and we're still getting our flavors worked out. I have plenty of savings to last at least half a year more, and if I'm not profitable by next summer, I was thinking of getting a part-time job at a natural foods store, or if things got really bad, I could always look for more hygienist work.

Mother seems to think that I should just settle down with some small town boy from Northfield, and give up my career aspirations. Well I'm sorry, Mother, but I actually really enjoy making marshmallows, and I think my business could take off. What if my path is to create the best artisan marshmallow company in California?

People could go to a store like Whole Foods and buy my products. If I give up now, I'll always be small-time, just another middle-aged baker at the farmers' market. Mother just doesn't seem to understand that I have greater aspirations than being a housewife, and wants me to move back to a snowy, depressing place like Northfield. There are many good reasons why I moved to San Diego, and the biggest one is her.

Oh, I almost forgot! I ran into Eric a little bit ago. Eric Robertson, the one who made the commemorative video, and my first boyfriend? Anyway, he arrived early to help set up the video, and I walked right past him – he's almost unrecognizable! I don't know if it was the divorce or perhaps the years have been kind, but he looks nothing like the chubby teddy bear I knew before.

He's still got a boyish face, but he's much fitter now, and actually more handsome than I remember, too. We got to talking a bit, and he's still the same in some ways (big, goofy laugh, and lopsided smile). I must've forgotten how blue his eyes were, though, or maybe it was just the shirt he was wearing. Anyway, it's not like I'm interested right now.

It turns out that Eric has a daughter who's in college, and of all places, she had her heart set on St. Olaf, here in Northfield. I guess her mother is a professor there, so they can get free tuition. His daughter is really into choir, especially a cappella, and St. Olaf is a great school for it. It means he doesn't get to see his daughter as often, which is why he wanted to bring her as his plus one to this party. Isn't that wild? Here I was, thinking he's already found a new girlfriend (he might've, with the way he's cleaned up), but the girl he was referring to was actually his daughter! She'll be here for the party later, so I'm looking forward to meeting her. I wonder if she resembles him more, or her mother.

Apparently Eric's been living in New York for the last fifteen years, working as a photographer. He's been doing a lot of studio work, like staged shoots for book covers, product photography, and some fashion photography. But his real passion is travel photography, and he said that he'd like to take his motorcycle on a cross-country tour someday, photographing everything along the way. It sounds very romantic, but after my recent experience on a motorcycle, I'm not sure that it would be as fun as it sounds.

I felt pretty silly when I found out that he lived in New York. This whole time, I assumed that he was still in Northfield! I should've looked at his website, at least. I hope I didn't say something offensive, since I assumed he was more into small-time jobs. I'll have to ask him about his work later, once the fundraiser is over.

Speaking of which, I'd better get back. We won't be opening for another 20 minutes, but you know how HHHA ladies are; always getting places half an hour early.

Gratitudes:
1. I am grateful that the party is today, because tonight it will be over.

TEXT MESSAGES, DECEMBER 24

Lisa:	hey can you let me in
Lisa:	i'm at the side entrance
Crystal:	??
Crystal:	i'm in northfield this week
Crystal:	are you trying to text someone else?
Lisa:	no i'm here for the HHHA party
Lisa:	nevermind someone else let me in
Crystal:	????
Crystal:	i thought you were doing the fontana christmas?

Lisa:	yeah tomorrow
Lisa:	today i'm cleaning up your mess
Crystal:	☹
Crystal:	i can't believe you flew all the way out here without telling me
Lisa:	i'd like to be in and out before mom sees me if possible
Lisa:	where's adam?
Crystal:	i told you i haven't seen him
Lisa:	we tracked him here
Crystal:	you can track him?
Lisa:	sort of...it's complicated
Crystal:	so he's here RIGHT NOW?
Lisa:	possibly
Crystal:	how can you be so calm?
Crystal:	shouldn't we evacuate or something?
Lisa:	no it's fine
Lisa:	we're doing a perimeter check
Lisa:	so stay put
Lisa:	where are you?
Crystal:	at the table by the flagpole
Crystal:	they're about to start the presentation
Crystal:	lisa?
Crystal:	OMG
Crystal:	YOU CAN'T SIT THERE
Lisa:	you don't have to shout i'm sitting right next to you

Crystal:	but THERE MIGHT BE A KILLER ROBOT ON THE LOOSE
Lisa:	relax boople has an ironclad extraction protocol
Lisa:	and adam can't kill anyone it's against his programming
Crystal:	that's what they always say in movies WHERE EVERYONE DIES
Crystal:	lisa?
Crystal:	why are you ignoring me?
Crystal:	and why do we have to text?
Lisa:	because it's rude to talk during a performance
Crystal:	WAIT
Crystal:	OMG are you PREGNANT?
Lisa:	no i just gained 40 pounds since i saw you last
Lisa:	of course i'm pregnant
Lisa:	stop gaping we have to keep this a secret from mom, remember?
Crystal:	boy or girl?
Lisa:	both
Crystal:	are you trying to be socially progressive or do you mean twins?
Lisa:	twins
Crystal:	congrats!!!!!!! :D :D :D
Lisa:	seriously stop staring
Lisa:	for the record i'm still mad at you
Crystal:	yeah but at least we're having a conversation again ☺
Lisa:	this is just a temporary truce for the HHHA party

Lisa:	because it's your fault i had to come all the way out here
Crystal:	OMG so all those times you were going to the dentist
Crystal:	YOU WEREN'T GOING TO THE DENTIST
Lisa:	well i couldn't exactly say i was going to the OB-GYN every other week
Lisa:	mom would've figured it out
Crystal:	did you plan this?
Lisa:	the kids?
Crystal:	of course the kids
Lisa:	yes and no
Lisa:	we were trying for a year before the miscarriage
Lisa:	but this was a bit of a shocker
Lisa:	you know how mom is
Lisa:	we didn't want her to get all excited and then put her through the heartbreak again
Lisa:	and if it did work out, she'd want to come visit all the time
Crystal:	might be a little hard to avoid that now
Crystal:	you're as big as a whale
Lisa:	says the girl dressed like a marshmallow
Crystal:	shut up i'm from southern california
Crystal:	i have every right to wear my puffer coat indoors
Crystal:	it's like minus four outside
Lisa:	celsius maybe
Crystal:	that's not the point
Crystal:	OMG is that grace and alice

Crystal:	dear god it's a mother-daughter tap dance
Crystal:	lisa you're missing it
Crystal:	look at the stage!!!
Crystal:	oh nooooo alice just tripped over a speaker cord!!!!
Crystal:	liiiiiissssaaaaaa
Crystal:	looooooooooook
Lisa:	he's here
Crystal:	what?
Lisa:	adam just arrived on his motorcycle
Crystal:	his motorcycle?
Crystal:	he DROVE here?
Lisa:	paul's going to try to calm him down
Crystal:	who's paul?
Lisa:	dr. paul devereux
Lisa:	he's an AI psychologist, and adam's handler
Crystal:	english please
Lisa:	crap it's not working
Lisa:	adam's heading our way
Crystal:	hey lisa
Crystal:	i think that's him
Crystal:	the guy beelining for the stage
Crystal:	lisa????
Lisa:	paul's switching to plan b
Crystal:	???
Lisa:	he's going to tell adam he's an android
Crystal:	0_o
Crystal:	we're doomed

BOOPLE SMART COMPANION ADAM DEVEREUX, LOG 000942, 12/24 20:22:03

Margot: Adam?

Adam: Margot, I—

Margot: Hang on. Rosalie, can you take the headset for a moment?

Rosalie: Is that—?

Margot: Thanks, Rosalie.

[SHUFFLING NOISES]

Margot: Alright, Adam. I've got five minutes. Hmm, make that four and a half.

Adam: Margot, I've been such a fool. I thought about what you said, and you're right. I was holding back, and I wasn't clear enough about how I feel. So I got on my bike and I drove straight here to tell you.

Margot: You drove from San Diego?

Adam: Yes, I can explain later. But right now, I need you to know how much I care about you. Before I met you, I tried to convince myself that loneliness was a fact of life, and that I should just accept it. But then I met you, and you were like a shining beacon of light, giving me a reason to jump out of bed every morning. Each day was a new adventure, and I counted the minutes until we saw each

	other again. When you told me that it was over, I couldn't understand it. And I've been thinking about what you said the whole way here, and I want to make it right.
Margot:	Adam...
Adam:	I want to be by your side, Margot, however you'll have me. If you want to be friends for now, that's fine. But I hope that someday, you might feel the same way that I do. I just can't let you go without a fight. Won't you give me a chance, Margot?
Margot:	[EXHALES] I've treasured the time we've spent together, Adam. We've had a great run, but I think it's time that we both admit that we're better off as friends. I still care about you, but I can't return your feelings. I truly appreciate you coming out here. That was incredibly courageous, and I'm so sorry, but it's just not going to work.

[SHUFFLING NOISES]

Paul:	Adam? Can I speak with you?
Margot:	Excuse me, but we're having a private conversation.
Adam:	*Dad?* What are you doing here?
Margot:	"Dad?"
Paul:	Adam, there's something I need to tell you.

[END TRANSCRIPT]

CRYSTAL'S JOURNAL, DECEMBER 25

I'm on a plane, flying back to San Diego. The HHHA fund-raiser was a disaster. It all started shortly after Lisa arrived.

She decided to fly out (in secret) with her colleague, Dr. Paul Devereux, who is also Adam's handler. Apparently they couldn't bring in a normal extraction team, because, as Lisa put it, I "bungled the whole thing up" and "made a fine mess of it." I still think it had something to do with the fact that Adam believed he was a human, because that definitely complicates things. But this didn't seem like the time to bring it up.

So Lisa and Paul had come to somehow extract Adam, since they'd used a variety of methods to track him here to Northfield. Paul tried to intercept Adam when he pulled up outside on his motorcycle (after driving it all the way from San Diego), but Adam didn't see him and beat Paul inside.

Lisa and I were having a nice little chat while watching the ridiculously cheesy commemorative video and accompanying mother-daughter tap dance routine (courtesy of Grace and Alice), when Adam burst in. He didn't interrupt the show, thankfully, but he went straight backstage to talk with Mom.

And I was pretty sure at this point that it wouldn't end well, but Adam looked more determined than murderous, which was a small consolation. So I tried to convince Lisa that we should go backstage to make sure Mom's okay, but she said that Paul was on it and if we went now, in the middle of the commemorative video, it might make a scene.

And then we started arguing, because I happened to mention that it looked like she wanted to sit tight just to avoid Mom, on account of the whole "let's keep Lisa's pregnancy a secret" thing. And then Lisa was like, "No it's because if Mom sees me like this she'll probably have a meltdown," and then I was like, "But she'll have a meltdown anyway,"...so yeah. It wasn't pretty.

Eventually Lisa finally admitted that there was a good reason that she didn't want Mom to know about the pregnancy, and it wasn't just about the miscarriage. "I'm afraid," she said. "I don't want to turn into her." And when I saw the look in her eyes, I understood immediately.

To be honest, it's something I'm afraid of every day. If I laugh a certain way or find myself using one of Mom's cheesy phrases, I realize just how much I'm like her, and it terrifies me to think of what else I might've absorbed, without even knowing it. And no matter how hard I try, she's always going to be a part of me, even some of the uglier parts.

But then I told Lisa that she shouldn't be afraid of turning into Mom, because she's her own person. And the best part about being a daughter is that you don't just absorb the bad parts, you get the good ones, too. Lisa's got Mom's determination, and she really cares about other people, just like Mom. I reminded Lisa that she turned out pretty well, so her kids probably will, too.

I think something clicked then for her, because Lisa said we should go backstage and find Mom. She thought we should be there to support her, because whatever happened next was bound to be rough. Mom was almost guaranteed to have a meltdown, but it was our fault (well, mostly mine, unfortunately), and it was time that we faced it – together.

The commemorative video finally finished, so we wove through the tables during the applause. As Lisa and I made our way backstage, I couldn't help but notice Grace and Alice near the stage stairs, having a hushed argument. I wasn't close enough to hear it, but I heard a sob, and saw Alice rushing away. I glued my eyes to the floor before Grace could see me gawking, but I did catch a glimpse of her expression, and she looked exhausted – and about five years older than I remembered.

Lisa and I arrived backstage and saw Paul and Mom and Adam standing there, and Mom and Adam had the strangest expressions on their faces.

"He's a *what?*" asked Mom, sounding more confused than shocked.

"He's an android," said Paul.

Adam's face was pale, and he was frozen in place.

Then Mom asked Paul if he had been drinking, and he tried to explain that he hadn't, and that he's an AI psychologist with Boople. He got out his business card and told Mom about the Smart Companion program.

Mom's face twitched, and then she said, "Does this have something to do with Lisa?"

And then Lisa skulked out from behind me, and Mom's eyes fell to her belly, and she murmured, "Don't tell me you're pregnant..."

Lisa nodded morosely, and then Mom hunched over, and she made this horrifying noise, possibly laughter or sobbing, or somewhere in the middle. Lisa and I just stood there, watching, waiting for The Meltdown, because there was no avoiding it. Any minute now, Mom was going to tell us that we were ungrateful and selfish. She was going to say that she didn't want to be "handled" and that we should've treated her with more respect. And the worst part was, this time, she'd be absolutely right. We'd gone too far.

But after a few moments, Mom looked up at Lisa and asked if Paul was telling the truth. But before Lisa could explain, I said that it was all my fault. I tried to tell her how sorry I was, and that Mom had said how she just wanted someone to be her companion, so when Lisa needed people to test their robots, it seemed like a good fit. And how it was really a terrible idea in retrospect, and how I was such an idiot...

Mom just listened, and she had this strange look on her face. Peaceful, almost. I've only seen her look that stoic a few times in my life, like the time we had to put our dog to sleep. And I was sure that she was going to tell us that she was done with all of us, with everything, and that we should all leave her alone. But she didn't. Instead, she said, "Well that explains a few things."

The look on Adam's face was heartbreaking. He shook his head, and then started shivering. "It's not true," he said. "I'm human."

I feel awful just thinking about it.

Paul walked over to Adam, and gently rolled up Adam's sleeve. Paul took a metal device out of his pocket and shined a light on Adam's arm. Paul put the device away and then, seconds later, a barcode and an alphanumeric code appeared beneath Adam's skin, as if lit from below.

Adam stared at his arm as if he didn't recognize it. Gone was the calm, grounded Adam we all knew. In his place was a frightened little boy, his eyes wide with fear.

Paul put a hand on Adam's shoulder, trying to gently lead him away. But then Margot was there, embracing him, and he sunk against her, sobs wracking his body.

Mom held Adam in her arms, a man twice her size who once seemed so strong, and invincible. I glanced at Lisa, but she was hanging her head in shame, feeling just as guilty as I did. Because both of us came into this preparing for a fight, readying our defenses against some imaginary meltdown. We assumed that Mom had reached her breaking point, and that she would crack under the pressure.

And yet here she was, finding strength from some invisible well, to support a man who was having the worst day of his life. Lisa and I had been so caught up worrying about our own guilt and our own punishments. Mom had every reason to be furious and hurt and betrayed, but instead she made herself a rock for Adam, whose entire world had just been shattered.

It's been so easy to complain about Mom and poke fun, but no matter how frustrating it was to be with her, Mom's intentions have always been pure. She might have been over-bearing or lonely or desperate, but that happens to the best of us.

I thought I could "fix" her by providing a companion. I lied to her and treated her like a child who had a problem to be solved, when all along, she was a much stronger woman than I had ever realized.

I don't know how long I stayed there, but at some point I came to my senses and realized that I had to get out of there. I stumbled out of the fundraiser, and caught a taxi to the airport. Now I'm on a plane headed for home, or at least the place I'll sleep for tonight, since I'm moving out of Mom's apartment as soon as possible. I'm not sure what happens next, but I've got a few ideas. I don't think I can face Mom again for awhile, and I'm not even sure how I'll begin to apologize. But I guess I've got some time.

What I do know is that I'm done lying. It's brought me nothing but trouble, and it's time that I come clean. Not just with Mom, but with David, too. I know it's a risk and I could lose him, but to be honest, he's been gone a long time, and I want to make sure that if we do get back together, we're starting off on the right foot.

God, I hope next Christmas is better than this one.

LETTER, RECEIVED DECEMBER 25

December 17

Hi Crystal,

I finally made it. It's almost surreal, but there it is. My ankle held up pretty well, and now I've officially walked from Canada to Mexico, all 2650 miles.

I called Mike as soon as I reached the marker, and I really wish he could've been there to see it with me. His mom is in the middle of chemo, and the doctor thinks she'll have a good chance of pulling through, since they caught it in the early stages.

Mom and Dad were there to pick me up at the border, and we're on our way back north. I've had a few good showers at least, and hopefully I'll be a little less scruffy by the time I see you again. I've been Smeagol for so long that I almost forgot what it's like to be David. The real world almost feels surreal, and even my sense of smell has changed. People smell artificially clean compared to the "trail funk" you get on the PCT.

I had some time to think about my future, and I've got some news to share with you. I'm looking forward to seeing you again, and hearing what you've been up to these last few weeks.

I've also enclosed a little present for you. I know it's not fancy, but it was the best I could do this year. There aren't a lot of malls on the PCT, so I hope you're ok with it.

I filled your sketchbook with all the animals I've seen along the trail, because they made me think of you. There are some you'll recognize, like the squirrels and the pika, but there are also some that I'd never seen before, like this fluffy bird (called a poorwhill). Unfortunately they don't have fennec foxes in the Mojave, but I did include a gray fox instead.

If you have time, I'd love to give you a call again soon. I should be back at my parents' place by New Year's.

-David

EMAIL, DECEMBER 26

From: Jennifer Smith <socks4days@booplemail.com>
To: Crystal Hemmingway <crystalkitty_01@booplemail.com>
Subject: Re: First three chapters

Hey Crystal,

Thanks for sending along your pages. I've attached a copy with my comments. I focused on broader points, as opposed to line edits, as you requested.

There's some good stuff there. Your writing is definitely coming along, and I could sense some genuine emotions in places. However, right now these first few chapters aren't quite working for me. It might just be a matter of taste, but it feels like

Rapunzel and Dame Gothel have a really complicated relationship, and I don't see much of the spark or humor that I hear from you normally. It's fine if you want to focus on writing a more serious and dramatic story, but from the way you initially described it, the story sounded like it was going to be more light-hearted.

I'm not sure if this helps at all, but that's just my take on it. Please don't be discouraged. I'd be happy to read more if you'd like, but also feel free to ignore my comments entirely. ;)

Jen

P.S. How about lunch next week?

EMAIL, DECEMBER 26

From: Steamy Reads Submissions <no-reply@steamyreads.com>
To: Crystal Hemmingway <crystalkitty_01@booplemail.com>
Subject: New and Novel Contest Closes 1/15

There are just 20 days left to submit your scorcher for the Steamy Reads New and Novel contest! Competition is fierce this year, so send us your best work. As always, don't forget to proofread. ;)

Steamy Reads Editorial Team

Steamy Reads: Fantasies to light up your night. Check out our latest addition, *Santa's Naughty Little Elf,* and stuff her stocking with the gift she really wanted.

LETTER, RECEIVED DECEMBER 27

Dear Mom,

I am so sorry for everything. I feel terrible about the Adam thing, and it's entirely my fault. Lisa was never in support of this plan, and she only found out about it when I asked for her help to end it. Please don't be mad at her, because this one is on me, and I take full responsibility for it.

I am so, so sorry for lying, and for keeping things from you. I didn't give you enough credit, and I am really sorry for hurting you. I really appreciated you taking me in when I was down, and giving me a place to write. Boople paid a stipend for the Smart Companion trial, and I tried to give you as much of the money as possible (without it being suspicious). I have included the remainder of the stipend, approximately $7,543, which I unjustly withheld until now.

I feel that the stipend was and always should have been yours, and so I'd like to pay you back for my half of the rent for the months that I stayed with you. I will begin payment in installments as soon as possible.

My presence seemed to cause you a lot of pain and grief, and I feel that it's time for me to move out again. I'm not trying to run away from my problems, but rather, to take some time to reflect on them and think about how I can make amends. Please accept the rent payments as a show of my good faith.

I'll send you my forwarding address as soon as I have a new apartment, which I expect will be within the next three weeks. In the meantime, you can reach me by phone or email in case of emergency.

I'm sorry again for all of the trouble, and I love you.
Crystal

LETTER, RECEIVED DECEMBER 27

Dear David,

Congratulations on finishing the PCT. That's an incredible accomplishment, and one that will stay with you for the rest of your life. I'm sure Mike was with you in spirit, and I'm glad that you had his company earlier on. I never would've expected that you'd take such a liking to the great outdoors.

Thank you also for the sketchbook. Your drawings are beautiful, as always, and I will cherish it. Thanks for your notations on the species as well – those poorwills are really fascinating little birds.

I had a rough holiday, to be honest. A lot of stuff came to light that had been hidden for a long time, and I think I messed up pretty badly. I can explain more on the phone, but basically, I wasn't treating Mom with the compassion that she deserved.

Because of that, and some other things, I wanted to make sure to come clean with you. I told myself that I didn't want to bother you with some of these things because you were on the trail, but in reality I was probably just scared. So before you read them, I'm sorry, but I really didn't know where we stood, so I'm doing my best to be brave and tell you now.

I was laid off from my job back in July, shortly after the Hawaii trip. Because of this, I soon ran out of money, and moved in with my mom in October. I was embarrassed about it, especially because I agreed with what you said about needing some distance from Mom, and it felt like the exact opposite of that. But she presented it as a way for me to write and keep my expenses low, and without any other roommates on the horizon, it seemed like the best option.

I would've felt better about the whole thing if I'd actually written something decent while I was there. I've been working for months on my Rapunzel novel, but I got hit with a bad case of writers' block. I sent some chapters to Jen for feedback, and what she said pretty much confirmed my fears. Even though it's some of my better writing, it's not fun or enjoyable to read. I think I was probably using it as a way to vent my frustrations, and it showed.

The worst part about it is that I'm not really sure where to go next. Jen suggested trying to write something with more humor to it, but I don't really know where to start.

Since Mom and I had that falling out over Christmas, I'm back in LA for the foreseeable future. I'm going to try to get a real job again, and probably start a new book on the side (once I have a decent idea). I'm not sure if any of my writing is actually worth reading, but I'm going to keep working on it, one word at a time.

I'm sorry again about keeping this from you. I really hadn't meant to deceive you; we were just out of touch for so long that it became harder and harder to tell you. I completely understand if you're upset with me, but I felt it was important to be straight with you.

Take Care,
Crystal

EMAIL, DECEMBER 28

From: David Richards <darth_david@booplemail.com>
To: Crystal Hemmingway <crystalkitty_01@booplemail.com>
Subject: Your Letter

Hey Crystal,

You don't need to apologize for moving back in with your mother. It was my fault that you didn't have the rent money, and I'm sorry that you were trying to hide it for my sake. I was in a bad place in Hawaii, and your mother was only one small part of it.

Jen's a harsh critic, so I wouldn't give up on your book because of her. You can always take a break from writing, or maybe just let off some steam. Didn't you write something funny a few years ago? I thought there was a dinosaur story you wrote for Lisa.

Let's talk soon.

-David

EMAILS, JANUARY 10

From: Eric Robertson <eric@ericrobertson.com>
To: Margot Hemmingway <margot.hemmingway@boople-mail.com>
Subject: Re: Margot's Mallows Website

Hi Margot,

Thanks for the kind words about my website and portfolio. It's been years in the making, and I had a great web designer.

Your Margot's Mallows website looks good, so I don't think you need to worry about redesigning it. It's not necessary to add wholesale prices or other information; it's generally better for people to request that from you directly. It's good to think about it, but since you already have a contact form, wholesalers will be able to reach you.

If you want to take it further, you'll want to look into really high quality photos. The images you have so far are good, but if you want to catch the eye of a major grocery chain like Whole Foods (as you said), professional photos will indicate a certain level of quality. I might be biased, but I've photographed my fair share of food, and the right image could make your marshmallows absolutely mouth-watering. There are probably some great people in San Diego when you're ready to take that step. To note, it's probably not worth getting professional photos until you've settled on your final or near-final packaging. I've had clients drop thousands on photos, which can make a product look amazing, but an inkjet printer label in HD is still an inkjet printer label. It's fine if you're not ready for that yet, but I highly recommend waiting until you're there before reaching out to the bigger health food stores.

My birthday was good, thanks for asking. I rode my motorcycle out to the Hamptons; my buddy has a house there. The beaches here aren't as warm as California, but we had a nice time out on the water. I've attached a couple of pictures; the sunrises were unbelievable. I think you would've enjoyed them. Have you ever been out that way?

Eric

BOOPLE CHAT, JAN 11 4:02 PM

Crystal:	heya
Lisa:	yo
Crystal:	how's work?
Lisa:	things are still a mess around here
Lisa:	only a few days left till they shutter our project
Crystal:	aw any word on the transfer?
Lisa:	not yet but i've got a good lead
Lisa:	so it's probably only a week or so now
Crystal:	that's good
Lisa:	might even be able to turn this into a promotion ;)
Crystal:	so there might be a silver lining after all?
Lisa:	don't push your luck
Crystal:	so did they give you guys a reason yet?
Lisa:	for shutting us down?
Crystal:	yeah
Lisa:	legal complications
Crystal:	oh god
Crystal:	everything ok?
Lisa:	yeah it has nothing to do with northfield ;)
Crystal:	what will happen to adam and the rest of them?

Lisa:	i've been trying to find out
Lisa:	so far it sounds like they're in the boople warehouse
Crystal:	like... in boxes? 0_o
Lisa:	no as workers
Crystal:	wow, really?
Crystal:	do they pay them?
Lisa:	dunno
Lisa:	but it's probably only a temporary solution
Crystal:	ah ok
Lisa:	how's the new gig?
Crystal:	eh it's not as fun as writing about princess playsets
Crystal:	but the instructions for these toasters will be ironclad
Crystal:	if one of our users burns their toast, it will NOT be my fault
Lisa:	LOL
Lisa:	are you talking to mom again yet?
Crystal:	not much
Crystal:	just sent her a check the other day
Lisa:	ah yeah she mentioned that
Crystal:	is she super excited about the baby?
Lisa:	omg yes
Lisa:	she's seriously going baby crazy
Lisa:	i think she sent us a dozen presents this week
Crystal:	oh wow
Crystal:	i hope it's nothing too expensive?

Lisa:	nah it's mostly necessities like formula...not designer bassinets
Crystal:	ah ok good
Crystal:	so what is everyone doing at work, when they're not looking for jobs?
Lisa:	some people stopped coming in altogether, because they gave us that option
Lisa:	i prefer to come in and scroll through facebook
Lisa:	my feed is filled with politics and babies these days
Crystal:	it's not just you
Crystal:	i'm getting babies all over my facebook too
Lisa:	ok this is going to sound really bad so don't judge me
Lisa:	but have you noticed how some babies are adorable and others are just...ugly?
Lisa:	they might grow up into perfectly fine-looking adults, but some of those babies...
Crystal:	oh you mean the ones that look like hairless monkeys?
Lisa:	yeah exactly
Crystal:	i have come to the earth-shattering realization that some babies are just Not Cute
Crystal:	it's not their fault, and usually their parents are plenty attractive
Crystal:	i think some people just get the short end of the stick in that department

Lisa:	or maybe their babies get swapped at the hospi-tal
Crystal:	i dunno
Lisa:	what if my babies are ugly? i won't just be stuck with one hairless monkey, i'm going to have TWO
Crystal:	aww you've got nothing to worry about
Crystal:	your babies are going to be the cutest
Lisa:	but you have no way of knowing that
Crystal:	i'm going to be their aunt, that's how i know
Lisa:	☺
Lisa:	how's the writing going?
Crystal:	i'm taking a break from the rapunzel novel
Crystal:	just need to think about something different for a while
Lisa:	like what?

VELOCIRAPTURE, PAGE 15

A piercing cry cut through the air. It was the mournful wail of a juvenile, likely a brachiosaurus calf who had wandered too far from the pack. Stella froze, sniffing the air. The other stegosauruses paid little heed; the cry was too far away to concern most of them. But Stella wasn't like the other herbivores. She was on the hunt – for a certain velociraptor.

She'd first spotted him a few days ago, when she'd wandered off in search of a particular fern. She caught his scent and held her tail poised, ready for an attack. But it was smaller prey that caught his interest that day, and Stella watched from the shadows as he calculated his attack, and leapt in for the kill. His speed was terrifying, and his claws cut with remarkable precision. And when his prey finally lay still, she watched in awe as he began to feed, pinning the creature beneath him.

Stella was frozen in place, and a surge of emotions rushed through her. An herbivore's life was so dull, so ordinary. Mosses and ferns were mute and willing prey. It was no wonder they left her feeling empty, no matter how many she ate. But here, watching this raptor gorge himself on living flesh, it was terrifying and intoxicating all at once. And, for a brief moment, Stella imagined that it was her pinned beneath the raptor, and that he was running his claw along her tender underbelly, keeping her on the tantalizing edge of pleasure and mortal pain.

The raptor must've caught her scent then, because he pulled back from the corpse, and his eyes sought out her own. Stella stumbled backward, frightened by the intelligence and intensity of his gaze. She felt heat rising in her plates as they flushed to a violent crimson, and she felt utterly exposed. Stella knew it was impossible, but it almost felt as if he could see straight into her heart, and that her forbidden lust was on full display. She turned and raced back to her pack, willing her plates to return to their usual soft tan.

He didn't follow, but part of her wished he did. And each day, that part grew stronger, until the memory of him left her moaning with desire each night. It was a lust that could never be sated; he was a predator, and her kind was prey. But her passion could not be quelled with reason, and her desire for him only increased with each passing day. Her daily routine became tiresome; her favorite ferns lost their flavor, and all she could think about was his intoxicating scent. She had to see him again. But how? Where?

Stella's raptor was no cocky tyrannosaurus, announcing his presence with each lumbering step. Raptors were smart; stealthy. He'd come like an assassin, dealing death with a swift and calculated strike. Her only hope was to follow the mortal cries of unlucky prey, because where there was death, there was a slim chance of finding him.

At the merest thought of their eventual meeting, she felt her cloaca tremble.

EMAIL, JANUARY 12

From: Margot Hemmingway <margot.hemmingway@booplemail.com>
To: Adam Devereux <adam_devereux@booplemail.com>
Subject: Hi from Margot

Hi Adam,

I don't know if you'll even be able to read this, but I wanted to send you a message, just in case. There are some things that I want to say, and I have to imagine that you will be able to hear me, even if it's just on an spiritual level.

I've been thinking of you a lot recently, and it's hard to believe that we only spent a few short weeks together. I really cherished the time we had, and our many adventures. You were always so kind to me, and you are such a caring person. I hope that wherever you are now, you are being treated well.

I'm so sorry about what happened on Christmas eve. It was a shock for me, too, and I think they could've told you in a more compassionate way. I want you to know that it doesn't change anything about the time we spent together. Our friendship was real, and it doesn't make you any less special than you already were. If anything, it only makes you more special. The Boople people might try to take credit for you, but you are your own person. It was you who laughed and listened and loved, and it was you who came up with so many brilliant ideas, including our best-selling chocolate-covered marshmallows.

And even though we might not have a romantic future, I will always consider you a dear and true friend. You are a remarkable person, Adam Devereux. I wish you all the best, and I hope that our paths will cross again someday.

Yours truly,
Margot

EMAIL, JANUARY 12

From: Dr. Paul Devereux <pdevereux@boople.com>
To: Lisa H. Fontana <lfontana@boople.com>
Subject: Re: Missing package

Hi Lisa,

I can't believe they lost one of your packages in the warehouse. It just goes to show that this campus has grown too large, and this type of negligence should not be tolerated.

I have a friend in the distribution department, so I'll have a chat with him today. Don't bother putting in a missing package request; he says they never have time to get to those anyway.

I'll keep you posted.

P

STEAMY READS NEW AND NOVEL CONTEST ONLINE APPLICATION, PAGE 2 OF 4

Q: Provide a brief description of your book.
A: Stella the Stegosaurus is a young herbivore who grows tired of her mundane life munching plants. When she stumbles upon an intimate scene of a velociraptor killing his prey, she is aroused for the first time, and becomes obsessed with him.

She soon leaves her pack, risking everything to sate her new-found dark appetite. Combining deadly dinosaurs with the allure of forbidden lust, *Velocirapture* provides a satisfying love story with many happy endings.

Q: What inspired you to write this story?
A: Honestly, I'm not exactly sure. I don't have sex fantasies about dinosaurs. I guess I just think dinosaur sex is funny, but it's still embarrassing to admit that I wrote a whole novel about it. Something is probably wrong with me.

Q: Name your favorite erotic fiction book.
A: I am an avid reader, but I don't actually read erotic fiction. However, I did flip through Athena Dale's *Steamed Buns* for reference. I originally saved it from my mom's donation pile as a joke, but I have a renewed respect for the author after attempting an erotic novel myself.

Q: Why should we choose your book?
A: I think readers will really enjoy the scene where Stella and the velociraptor indulge in some hardcore S&M foreplay in the oasis. Her cries of mingled pain and pleasure are so convincing that they attract a flock of starving *Compsognathus*. I believe that this scene illustrates the great depth of unexplored possibilities within the genre.

EMAIL, JANUARY 13

From: Margot Hemmingway <margot.hemmingway@boople-mail.com>
To: Eric Robertson <eric@ericrobertson.com>
Subject: Labels galore

Hi Eric,

So glad that you enjoyed the marshmallow sampler. I can see why the chocolate-covered original flavor gets your vote; they seem to be selling out each week.

I've attached the sample labels from my graphic designer. Which do you think looks more professional: the yellow or the blue? He said we could also add multiple colors, but I already bought 1000 yards of blue ribbon, so I'm leaning toward the blue.

I've also included some links to local food photographers below. They seemed to do good work, but one is quite a bit more expensive than the others. Do you think he's worth it?

I'll be out of town this weekend, so apologies in advance if you don't hear back from me for a few days. Hope that your magazine photoshoot goes well. I imagine it's a lot of work to wrangle models in giant dresses into moving helicopters, but I'm sure it'll be stunning. I can't wait to see the results!

Thanks,
Margot

EMAIL, JANUARY 13

From: Dr. Paul Devereux <pdevereux@boople.com>
To: Lisa H. Fontana <lfontana@boople.com>
Subject: Re: Missing package

Hi Lisa,

Good news! My buddy in distro has a lead on your missing package. There might be some paperwork involved, but if you swing by sometime late Monday, after the dinnertime rush, he should be able to have you in and out in 15 minutes or so.

Coffee later?

P

EMAIL, JANUARY 13

From: Order Fulfillment <mike@hardware4hobbyists.com>
To: Lisa Hemmingway <nsyncfan1999@hotmail.com>
Subject: Your order has shipped!

The following items have shipped:
- Black one hole balaclava ski mask, adult small, Qty. 1
- Black one hole balaclava ski mask, adult medium, Qty. 1

- Black one hole balaclava ski mask, adult x-large, Qty. 12
- Aluminum hand truck with pneumatic wheels, Qty. 6
- Duct tape original, Qty. 6
- Mini stun gun w/built-in alarm and flashlight 46 million volts, pink, Qty. 12
- Glass marbles bulk lot, 500 count, Qty. 3
- Great Outdoors rectangle Big and Tall sleeping bag, 30F, Qty. 6 – FINAL SALE

Your items were shipped using:

ONE DAY RUSH SHIPPING (1 business day)

Click here for tracking information.

Thank you for shopping with Hardware 4 Hobbyists, LLC. *It's Not Just a Hobby!*

CRYSTAL'S JOURNAL, JANUARY 14

When I got home from work today, I found Mom standing outside my door. I don't know how she got my address; I can only assume that Lisa gave it to her. It would've been nice if she'd at least given me a heads up, because I was really not prepared for this, especially after another mind-numbing day writing manuals for people who don't know that water and electricity don't mix.

Of course I let Mom in, especially because she had the most pitiful look on her face. She said that she hadn't been waiting long, but honestly, I wouldn't want anyone waiting on my doorstep for more than a few minutes. I can't afford to live in the nice part of town anymore, and I have a brutal commute to this tiny studio out in the valley.

I offered Mom a glass of water, and she accepted. We hadn't spoken a word to each other in weeks, so we retreated to the safety of small talk. I could see the judgment in Mom's eyes when she looked around at my dingy apartment, but when she looked back at me, her expression was kind.

And before I could think, I blurted out an apology, and then Mom held me in her arms and shushed me, and told me that she was sorry, too. She said that she had been upset before, but not now. "I could never stay mad at you," she said. "Because you're my daughter." And that's when I began to sob, and pretty soon Mom was sobbing too.

For a moment, it was enough that she was there with me, and telling me everything was going to be ok. Because, no matter what has come between us, there's no one quite like my mother. She might be emotional sometimes or irrational or needy, but she's still my mother, and I will always love her, even if I don't always show it in the ways she wants.

So we just sat with each other for awhile, talking and laughing a bit, and finally the awkwardness had melted away. She told me that she was proud of me, even now, for standing on my own two feet. She said that she would always be there if I needed her, but she understood that I wanted my own life, my own place.

But eventually we couldn't tiptoe around the difficult things anymore. Mom started to say how she wants me to be honest, and to be confident in who I am. Then she said, "Your happiness is my happiness and it hurts that you felt you had to lie to me." I could feel the tears welling up again, but I pushed them away. I apologized again, and said that I wasn't going to lie anymore.

Now Mom is sleeping in my bed and I'm on the couch, but I can't sleep just yet. I feel so much better now; lighter. It's not like I needed Mom's approval to live on my own, but I'm glad that she came today. I used to take it for granted that she'd always be there to support me. There've been so many times when she talked incessantly and I was in desperate need of some alone time. But the funny thing was, when we weren't talking, I really missed her.

EMAIL, JANUARY 15

From: Leo Brooks <leo@gatewaygames.com>
To: David Richards <darth_david@booplemail.com>
Subject: Lead Level Design opportunity

Hey David,

We heard great things about your work on *MOB2*. One of your colleagues, Colin Walsh, thought you might be a good fit for our Lead Level Design position. As our project is unannounced, we can't say too much about it, but it's an action-adventure title set in a vast, sprawling world. We offer competitive pay, full benefits, and strive for a work/life balance.

We're looking to move fast on this position, and we recognize that New York can have a high cost of living, so we're willing to offer a guaranteed pay raise of at least 50% over your current salary, with further opportunities for advancement. We also have a great relocation package, as many of our devs can attest. Hope to hear from you soon.

Leo

EMAIL, JANUARY 15

From: Lisa H. Fontana <lfontana@boople.com>
To: Dr. Paul Devereux <pdevereux@boople.com>
Subject: Re: Missing package

You free now? Swing by my desk whenever you're ready. Let's stop for coffee on the way there.

Lisa

EMAIL, JANUARY 20

From: Steamy Reads Submissions <no-reply@steamyreads.com>
To: Crystal Hemmingway <crystalkitty_01@booplemail.com>
Subject: New and Novel Contest Submission

Dear Crystal,

Congratulations! Your novel, "Velocirapture," has been selected as the grand prize winner in the Steamy Reads New and Novel contest. Steamy Reads would like to offer you a publication deal, starting with a $10,000 cash prize (as detailed in the attached documents). Please review the attached documents and return by January 22.

We'll also require your RSVP for the awards banquet, which will be held January 27 in New York City. As the grand prize winner, Steamy Reads will cover your airfare* and hotel, should you choose to accept the prize.

Congratulations,
Steamy Reads Editorial Team

Steamy Reads: Fantasies to light up your night. Check out our latest addition, *Extra Meaty: A Sub Shop Romance*, and lunch will never be boring again.

Full airfare is covered for any of the contiguous 48 states. Other destinations will be awarded a flight voucher, as explained in the attached paperwork.

EMAIL, JANUARY 24

From: Eric Robertson <eric@ericrobertson.com>
To: Margot Hemmingway <margot.hemmingway@booplemail.com>

Subject: Re: Margot's Mallows Website

Hi Margot,

Wow! That's great to hear that you'll be carried in one of the local co-ops. That's a great way to build exposure, and get your product out in front of passionate people who are likely to be your biggest advocates. Getting in the first store is always the hardest; the rest should get easier.

Now is the perfect time to invest in those photos, because you never know when Whole Foods will come knocking. Honestly, I think the photographers in your area are overpriced for what they offer. So I had a proposal for you. I'm long overdue for a vacation, and I've got a couple of weeks before my next shoot. It seems like the perfect time to do my cross-country ride, and it would be great if I could enjoy a couple of days somewhere sunny and warm first, like, say, San Diego. It would be no trouble to bring my portable light kit, and we could knock out those photos in a couple of hours, on me.

What do you say?
Eric

EMAIL, JANUARY 24

From: Kim Freeman <kfreeman@steamyreads.com>
To: Crystal Hemmingway <crystalkitty_01@booplemail.com>
Subject: Re: New and Novel Contest Submission

Hi Crystal,

I was able to get you booked on a direct flight on the 26th, but the only seat they had left was in first class. One of our editors is friends with a guy at Delta, so enjoy the extra legroom. ☺ I hear they serve cookies on the afternoon flights, but I wouldn't know from experience LOL.

I've attached a copy of the itinerary and flight information, but let me know if you have any questions.

See you soon,
Kim

P.S. Have you ever considered writing a sequel?

Steamy Reads: Fantasies to light up your night. Check out our latest addition, *Massive Balls: A Regency Romance*, and she'll be swooning this Valentine's Day.

CRYSTAL'S JOURNAL, JANUARY 29

This weekend has been a whirlwind. I just got back from New York, and my head is spinning, but I wanted to get it all down before I forgot anything.

I decided to accept the grand prize award for *Velocirapture*, and part of the deal was that I was supposed to attend an awards banquet in New York. I thought it was going to be some small thing in a little hotel conference room or something, and that I'd get a couple of days in New York out of it, but boy, was I happy to be wrong. New York is pretty crazy, but there's this girl named Kim from Steamy Reads who is super nice, and she gave me some great recommendations for vegetarian restaurants and stuff. So I got some awesome food and did a little shopping on Saturday, and then got ready for the banquet on Saturday night.

And oh my god, it was this big thing with all these romance writers and stuff. Not just Steamy Reads people, or even ero people, but like an entire community of people who write romance. To be honest, I was pretty nervous, and when I saw how many people were there, I wanted to turn right back to my hotel. But then Kim found me, and she was so sweet, and she introduced me to the Steamy Reads team. And all of them had read the book, since they were the judges, and they were all gushing about it.

It was pretty embarrassing, to be honest. But when they started talking about the character development for the velociraptor and Stella's repressed desires, it actually turned into a pretty interesting discussion. Some of the editors even had a couple of ideas for small things we could change before publishing, and I was completely on board. It was kind of funny, actually, because I began to see how there's a real art to writing a good sex scene, and there's still so much more for me to learn.

Anyway, the whole thing went well, and when it was time to go up and accept the award, I somehow forgot to be nervous. The Steamy Reads team was so nice and the whole night just felt kind of surreal. People I hadn't even met were congratulating me, and not in a joking way, either. I feel kind of silly for saying this, but I guess I always thought ero fiction was something to be embarrassed about. I didn't realize that people can take it so seriously as a career, and it made me think that this might not be such a bad idea for a day job, after all. If I can write another decent one, that is.

Ok so it gets even crazier because I happened to mention that I was going to New York to David, and he said that he was going to be there through Tuesday. We'd been trying to find a time to get together, but he had this job interview come up at the last minute and so we decided just to meet in New York.

It was strange seeing him again, after all this time. He looked leaner, a little more tan, and his hair was slightly different (longer, maybe?). Anyway we've been talking a bit since New Year's so it wasn't too awkward, but it did feel strange to be around him again.

He'd been interviewing for a lead game design job at a really swanky studio in NYC. It sounded like an amazing opportunity – a beautiful workplace, a lot of smart, talented coworkers, and a game that was more of an adventure, which is one of his favorite genres. The more he talked about it, the more excited he seemed to get, and I started to get this horrible feeling in the pit of my stomach. Because it was a fantastic opportunity, and I didn't want to hold him back. It sounded like the studio was really courting him, and they made him an offer he'd be stupid to refuse. So I was sure that this would be the end, and that David was just trying to give me a proper goodbye.

So I asked him if he accepted, and he said that it seemed like the right thing to do, because on paper it was everything he wanted. But as they talked about things like the work/life balance, saying how they cap people at 60 hour weeks, the whole thing just started to feel wrong. Because working 60 hours isn't a balanced lifestyle. It's five 12-hour days or six 10-hour days, plus commute time. There'd be no time to exercise, or eat healthy. Then he laughed, and said that people on the PCT kept saying "the trail gets inside you," but he really didn't understand it until now. "I just can't live my life like that anymore," he said. "There's no time to just 'be.'"

He said that he had this idea on the trail, about creating a game that really captured the essence of an adventure, in the old-fashioned, romantic sense. There are dozens of "adventure" games on the market, but most of them are mostly just action games, or sandboxes. "I want to build a game that captures what it feels like to be in a forest," he said. "Or how it feels to be alone in the desert, watching a blazing sunrise." And he already had some ideas for how he can do it.

I told him that I thought it was a great idea, and that he should go for it. He said that most people would probably think he was crazy to attempt something like this, especially with almost no savings. But he plans to work part-time at an outdoor gear store, since he picked up quite a few tips about camping and hiking. He hasn't decided where he wants to be based yet, but for his game project, he can live almost anywhere.

So then he asked about the banquet, and I told him that it was really nice, and that I really got along with the Steamy

Reads people. I said that I was actually proud to get up on that stage and accept the award, even though it was a story I'd written as a joke that got me there. David was really encouraging too, which kind of surprised me. He's such an intellectual and loves things like Tolkien. I didn't realize that he'd take this kind of thing seriously. But he actually said he was proud of me, and it made me smile, because those words still remind me of Mom.

David had some free time before his flight back, so he suggested that we stop by this really cool vegetarian restaurant nearby. It was super tasty, and it almost felt like old times. But then David set off in a taxi to fly back to his parents' place, and I was left wondering if it was all just a wonderful dream. For some reason, I had this foolish idea that we'd see each other, the sparks would fly and BAM! it'd be back to the way it was.

But we can't go back to the way it was. We've both grown and changed, and for the better, I think. It would be really nice if David and I could be together again (if our pseudo-date was any indication, the sparks are still there), but I just don't know if that's possible. David finally found something he's really passionate about doing, and I don't want to hold him back. As for me, I'm still an amateur ero writer, living in a dingy apartment in the valley until I can make enough to quit my day job.

It's probably hopeless, but I think part of me always imagined that, after all this, David and I would be together again. I know I'm alright on my own, but when I was with David today, the world felt a little brighter again.

EMAIL, FEBRUARY 8

From: Peggy Hemmingway <phemmingway@hhha.org>
To: Margot Hemmingway <margot.hemmingway@boople-mail.com>
Subject: Marshmallows?

Dear Margot,

How is San Diego? Still lots of snow in Northfield...mostly slush now.

Have you given up on marshmallows? Grace said you weren't at the farmers' market yesterday. Heard she and Alice had a falling out...hope they can patch it up soon.

Are Lisa's little ones still in the oven?

Love you much.
Mother

CRYSTAL'S JOURNAL, FEBRUARY 13

Lisa went into labor last night. She said that she didn't want anyone to fly in, but then she was having trouble reaching Mom, and sounded kind of panicked. So I called in sick at work and got on a plane, and managed to get there just as it ended.

Lisa and Bryan are now the proud parents of two healthy little babies, Quentin and Kayla Fontana. And for the record, they're pretty cute (for babies). I'd still be more excited about kids if they were as cute as kittens, but that's beside the point.

I'm an aunt now.

Hopefully that means I get to be a "cool" aunt, and not some cheek-pinching terror. But I guess that's mostly up to me.

When Lisa asked if I wanted to hold one of them, I was pretty nervous. I'm not good with babies, and I'm always afraid that I'm going to drop them. But Lisa showed me where to put my hands and how to support Kayla's little head, and she was actually kind of sweet. You know, for a pudgy little newborn.

We're still not sure what's going on with Mom, but Eric was coming to visit this week, so I'm pretty sure that she's just busy with… things I'd rather not be thinking about. It could be something simple, like if she lost her phone, but I was honestly kind of surprised that she'd drop out of touch at a time like this. The kids were a little early, but still.

Lisa's been pretty calm today, and she seems quite a bit relieved now that the kids have arrived safely. It sounds like it was a lot of stress to get things set up at her new job (still at Boople, but a more senior position). Lisa organized it all so she could drop everything when the kids came. She's got the next few months all planned out, like how she and Bryan are staggering their parental leaves so they can be together the first few weeks, and then alternate over the next couple of months.

I also casually mentioned how I finally finished *Velocirapture*, and how it happened to win the contest. Lisa was kind of miffed that I hid it from her until now, but once I gave her a printed copy, all was forgiven.

And then Bryan said Lisa had a visitor, and this tall guy walked in. He had blue eyes and blonde hair poking out of a baseball cap, with a scattering of stubble. There was something about him that looked startlingly familiar. He was middle-aged and quite handsome – not exactly someone I'd expect to be in Lisa's inner circle of friends.

But Lisa introduced him as Dave, a barista at her favorite coffee shop. When we shook hands, he winked at me, and then recognition dawned in me. Of course I knew him. His hair was different, his clothes were more casual, but it was him alright: our Adam.

I gaped at Lisa, and she started laughing at me.

"Does Mom know?" I asked.

"No, we want to surprise her," she said.

It was nice to catch up a bit with Adam. He and Lisa told the harrowing tale of how she and Paul had smuggled all the Smart Companions out (with the help of an intrepid distribution center employee). It was Lisa's idea, but Paul insisted on taking the blame, since he claimed he was "long past the age where he should retire, anyway." Boople went to great lengths to keep it under wraps, and they still don't have a clue that Lisa was involved.

Lisa and Bryan took Adam in, updating his appearance with some hair dye and a new sense of fashion. They got him a job at the coffee shop through a friend of Bryan's, and now Adam has a place of his own. But he's not planning to be a barista forever – he's been working on a new screenplay, and he plans to shop it around when it's done. He knows it'll be a long shot, but he's going to try.

I'm so happy for Lisa, and her family. It's great that they can see Adam now and then, and that he's finally able to live for himself. But when I left the hospital today, I couldn't help feeling a little down. Lisa has Bryan, and now Adam/Dave has a dream. Mom is off with Eric probably, and then there's me, going home to an empty, crappy apartment. I might have a $10,000 check in the mail, but it won't keep me warm at night, or pay my L.A. expenses for long.

I'm not depressed about it, but it just seems like everyone else is off doing what they do best, and I've got to claw my way up again. I'm really grateful that I get to publish *Velocirapture*, but it's only the beginning of another long journey.

EMAIL, FEBRUARY 14

From: Margot Hemmingway <margot.hemmingway@boople-mail.com>
To: Crystal Hemmingway <crystalkitty_01@booplemail.com>, Lisa H. Fontana <lisa.fontana@booplemail.com>
Subject: Congratulations, Lisa!

Hi Girls,

Congratulations, Lisa! I just saw a picture of darling little Quentin and Kayla. I'm so glad you are all doing well and couldn't be a prouder Grandma.

Sorry that I couldn't fly out for the birth – I left my phone at home – oops! I'm on the road with Eric, and we're riding across the country, back to his home in New York City. We're in Indianapolis now, and are about two days out. Once I get there, I'll get straight on a plane to see the grandbabies!

I've got some big news of my own. Eric asked me to marry him! It was so romantic – he took me for a hot air balloon ride, and as we were flying over the city, he got down on one knee. He said that he "just knew" when we met again at Christmas, and didn't want to let me get away. There were some happy tears, so that's why my face is a little red in the photo.

See you soon, Lisa! Love you both!
Mom

TEXT MESSAGES, FEBRUARY 14

David:	hey crystal
David:	how do you feel about weddings?
Crystal:	like weddings in general or a hypothetical wedding in which i would be getting married?
David:	the second one
Crystal:	same as always
Crystal:	they're super expensive and planning one would be a PITA
Crystal:	and there's no way i could have one without mom being super involved

David:	cool that's what I thought
Crystal:	?
David:	ok look out your window
Crystal:	is this some kind of joke?
David:	just look
Crystal:	OMG what are you doing here????
David:	come outside and find out

BOOPLE CHAT, FEB 15 2:41 PM

Lisa:	oh good you're back
Lisa:	did you see mom's email?
Crystal:	yeah
Lisa:	at first i was like WTF
Lisa:	she just met the guy
Crystal:	well yes and no
Crystal:	she dated him in high school
Crystal:	for like two years i think
Lisa:	that was decades ago
Lisa:	and two years in high school is like two days in real life
Crystal:	:/
Crystal:	depends on the relationship i guess
Lisa:	from the sound of it, they barely held hands before
Crystal:	but they were compatible at least
Crystal:	mom said they've been emailing

Crystal:	sounds like he's been giving her good business advice
Crystal:	you saw that she got her marshmallows into that co-op, right?
Lisa:	yeah it's a start
Lisa:	but seriously...marriage?
Crystal:	i dunno, i really think this one is up to her
Crystal:	if she's not 100% sure they can always have a long engagement
Lisa:	hmm true
Lisa:	not to be nosy
Lisa:	but how are things going with david?
Crystal:	:D
Crystal:	i was going to wait to tell you on the phone, but...
Crystal:	WE GOT MARRIED :D :D :D
Lisa:	WHAT??????????????
Crystal:	yeah we eloped
Lisa:	and you didn't invite me????
Crystal:	well if i did then mom would've felt left out
Crystal:	so it was just me and david and barfbag
Lisa:	barfbag?
Crystal:	that's his trail name, david met him on the PCT
Crystal:	i don't remember his real name, but he's a justice of the peace
Lisa:	you got married by a guy named barfbag and you didn't invite me?
Crystal:	i'm sorry but we just wanted to be married and not have all the hoopla

Crystal:	you know what mom's like
Lisa:	yeah
Crystal:	oh and one more thing
Crystal:	mom seems pretty stoked right now and i don't want to spoil it
Crystal:	so do you mind keeping the whole elopement thing between us?
Lisa:	she's going to find out eventually
Crystal:	yeah but just for a few days at least
Lisa:	alright, but no more secrets, ok?
Crystal:	says the woman with the renegade robot buddy

EMAIL, FEBRUARY 23

From: No Goat Soap <alice@nogoatsoap.com>
Bcc: Margot Hemmingway <margot.hemmingway@booplemail.com>
Subject: Save the Goats

Dear Conscious Consumer,

It is with great sadness that I must inform you that your favorite soap company, Grateful Goats Soaps, is a business built on lies and propaganda. The owner has led you to believe that her products are helping the goats of Nepal, and the soaps are produced by her own hands.

This couldn't be further from the truth.

Grateful Goats Soaps are manufactured by underpaid children in China, and there are no regulations for how this goats' milk is produced. Thousands of goats are orphaned – or killed – each year in the production of this supposedly "sustainable" and "organic" product.

Fortunately, there is an alternative.

When I learned of the cruelty behind Grateful Goats Soaps, I began an exhaustive search for a truly sustainable and organic bar soap. I came up empty-handed, so I began making my own soaps in my kitchen from the best ingredients I could find. After weeks of testing, I finally have created the perfect soap: No Goat Soap.

Created from coconuts harvested by generously-paid workers in Thailand, No Goat Soap has all the creaminess of a traditional goats' milk soap without any of the negative consequences. It is organic, vegan, and gluten-free. Each batch is made with my own hands, and I have the burns to prove it. Absolutely no goats are harmed in the making of the soaps, and all proceeds from our sales benefit the Nepalese baby goat sanctuary.

As a conscious consumer, I know you will make the right choice.

-Alice
Owner of No Goats Soaps

Find us at the farmers' market each Sunday, across from Grateful Goats Soaps.

PRESS RELEASE, APRIL 8

FOR IMMEDIATE RELEASE

ALEXANDRIA FILMS TO PRODUCE "HELP! MY GIRLFRIEND IS A ROBOT!"

Alexandria Films has announced plans to produce "Help! My Girlfriend is a Robot!", a feature film starring Triston Hardy and Mia Murray.

In "Help! My Girlfriend is a Robot!", Darien Sloan (Hardy) is a hardworking video game programmer who is tired of dating high-maintenance women. Suddenly, the girl of his dreams appears. Darien begins dating Poppy Jones (Murray), a naturally beautiful, intelligent, hardworking woman, who also happens to be the perfect housewife. The only problem? She's secretly a robot.

"We produced a lot of gritty, emotional dramas last year," said Sydney Patel, Director of Production at Alexandria Films. "We felt it was time for something lighter, and more fun. 'Help! My Girlfriend is a Robot!' has the perfect blend of romance, comedy, and action, while still remaining grounded in genuine character drama."

"Help! My Girlfriend is a Robot!" is a feature-length romantic comedy, directed by Joe Black ("Fiddlesticks") and written by newcomer Dave Gleason. Principal photography will begin in October in Los Angeles.

EMAIL, MAY 2

From: Crystal Hemmingway <crystalkitty_01@booplemail.com>
To: Debra Garza <dgarza@steamyreads.com>
Subject: Velocirapture Query

Hi Debbie,

I just completed my 65,000 word manuscript, *Velocirapture 2: Tyrannosaurus Sex*, as you requested. *Velocirapture 2* is the tale of a sexually repressed young tyrannosaurus, who lusts after Stella the Stegosaurus, the saucy herbivore who sated her carnal desires with a fearsome velociraptor in the original novel. Stella is now an outcast from her pack, and, after the tragic drowning of her conquest, she wanders the plains defending herself from predators such as the great tyrannosaurus. With five steamy sex scenes and exotic settings including tar pits, salt flats, and volcanic hot springs, *Velocirapture 2* is sure to delight dinosaur fetishists and general audiences alike.

Hope you enjoy it,
Crystal

BOOPLE CHAT, MAY 5 3:22 PM

David:	i just finished reading your draft
David:	and i have a very serious question for you
Crystal:	ok, shoot
David:	am i the velociraptor or the t-rex?
Crystal:	hmmmmm
Crystal:	i'll tell you tonight ;)

ABOUT THE AUTHOR

Crystal Hemmingway is a corporate washout and novelist. She lives in Los Angeles with her favorite person and two cats. In her spare time, Crystal enjoys binge-watching TV shows, eating sugary cereals, and pretending to write at coffee shops. Visit Crystal online at www.crystalhemmingway.com and follow her on Goodreads.

ONE LAST THING...

Yay! You reached the end of the book! Since I'm not there to thank you in person, I drew you a dopey dinosaur:

But seriously, it means the world to me that you took the time to pick up this book and read it. You're the best. Truly.

If you have any thoughts on the book, I'd love to get your opinions through honest reviews. Even a sentence or two on Amazon would be a huge help. Your thoughts can have a big impact on other readers, and you can help others find their next great read (or send them running, if they don't like dinosaurs, marshmallows, and other ridiculousness). I regularly read reviews, and use them to help improve my future books.

Also, if you have any friends or family (or coworkers or vague acquaintances) who might enjoy this novel, you'd totally make my day if you told them about it (or gifted it to them, if you're feeling extra generous).

To be the first to know about my upcoming books, sign up for my (very rare) newsletter on www.crystalhemmingway.com, or follow me on Instagram, Twitter, Goodreads, or Amazon Authors.

Thanks again, Crystal

Looking for a
Book Club Guide?

Get your **FREE** printable Reading Group Guide:

https://galbadiapress.com/book-club/

Galbadia Press is here to support your book club! We offer:

- A printable Reading Group Guide, including discussion questions and author Q&A
- Event ideas, such as a marshmallow exchange, soap-making party, themed wine tasting, or crafting PCT love letters
- Phone interviews with the author
- Bulk book discounts
- Need-based sponsorships
- Autographed bookplates, bookmarks and other promotional items

For any book club requests, email press@galbadiapress.com

Are you reading Mom's Perfect Boyfriend? *Let us know! Send pictures to* press@galbadiapress.com *or tag @galbadiapress on Instagram or Twitter and you could be featured on our social media!*

CPSIA information can be obtained
at www.ICGtesting.com
Printed in the USA
LVHW041624020719
623003LV00016B/971/P